Dead Start

"I want to make this mob into a military force," Daniel said. "Train it, arm it, and send it against Lamarine to blow that supply dump. Do that, at the same time you blow the rest, and the Machists are *our* prisoners until the Combine comes to our liberation."

A strange gleam flashed in Sten Rolvag's eye, one that hinted at madness. "So you want to train my people to blow up Lamarine," he said warily.

"That's right," Daniel replied. "I don't see why——"

At that moment, under the table, Rolvag pulled his pistol and fired. The action caught Daniel completely by surprise. He moved forward in reflex action, and the beam caught him full, bathed him. He was frozen for a second, then flared and winked out.

It was a total annihilation. A helluva way to begin an important mission . . . but then beginnings *were* always rough . . .

Dancers in the Afterglow

Jack L. Chalker

A Del Rey Book

BALLANTINE BOOKS • NEW YORK

This book is for all those people who will read it and still wonder where those stories come from.

al·ien (āl′yən, ā′lē ən), *n.* **1.** one born in or belonging to another country who has not acquired citizenship by naturalization (distinguished from *citizen*). **2.** a foreigner. **3.** one who has been estranged or excluded. **4.** a nonterrestrial being. —*adj.* **5.** residing under a government or in a country other than that of one's birth without having or obtaining rights of citizenship there. **6.** belonging or relating to aliens: *alien property*. **7.** foreign; strange; not belonging to one: *alien speech*. **8.** adverse; hostile; opposed (usually fol. by *to* or *from*): *ideas alien to our way of thinking*. **9.** nonterrestrial. [ME < L *aliēn(us)*, equiv. to *ali(us)* other + *-ēnus* adj. suffix; see -ENE] —**Syn.** **1.** immigrant. **2.** See **stranger**. **3.** outcast.

al·ien·age (āl′yə nij, ā′lē ə-), *n.* **1.** state of being an alien. **2.** the legal status of an alien. Also called **alienism**. [ALIEN + -AGE]

al·ien·ate (āl′yə nāt′, ā′lē ə-), *v.t.,* **-at·ed, -at·ing. 1.** to make indifferent or averse; estrange: *He has alienated his entire family.* **2.** to turn away; transfer or divert: *to alienate funds from their intended purpose.* **3.** *Law.* to transfer or convey, as title, property, or other right, to another: *to alienate lands.* [late ME < L *aliēnāt(us)* (ptp. of *aliēnāre*), equiv. to *aliēn(us)* ALIEN + *-ātus* -ATE¹] —**al′ien·a′tor,** *n.*

al·ien·a·tion (āl′yə nā′shən, ā′lē ə-), *n.* **1.** act of alienating. **2.** state of being alienated. **3.** *Law.* a transfer of the title to property by one person to another; conveyance. **4.** *Psychiatry.* **a.** mental or psychiatric illness. **b.** legal insanity. **5.** *Statistics.* the lack of correlation in the variation of two measurable variates over a population. [late ME < L *aliēnātiōn-* (s. of *aliēnātiō*), equiv. to *aliēnāt(us)* (see ALIENATE) + *-iōn- -*ION]

al·ien·ism (āl′yə niz′əm, ā′lē ə-), *n.* **1.** alienage. **2.** the study or treatment of mental diseases, esp. in their relation to legal problems. [ALIEN ·|· -ISM]

Portamento

THE END OF THE WORLD HAPPENED OUT OF SIGHT AND out of mind.

Umi-jada! Umi-jada! Wamma, wamma bing bang!

The dancers form in a semblance of a line, and step in and out, to and fro, to the music of an exotic steel band.

Jami-bobba, jami-bobba, rama zama ding dong!

Overhead, a light-year or so from the planet Ondine where the dancers ignorantly revel, worried commanders examine war-board screens in great battle cruisers.

Umi-jada! Umi-jada! Wamma, wamma bing bang!

The man looks at the ersatz chorus line with longing and some wry amusement, leaning back on his bar stool, sipping Ondinian ale.

Jami-bobba, jami-bobba, rama rama ring rang!

"*Dagger*'s completely out, sir," a young officer reports to the admiral aboard the flagship. The commander is about thirty years older than his chronological age, and reaches for a stomach pill, gulps it down with some water.

"We can't hold the line without her," the old man manages to utter in a voice hoarse and strained. The aide looks uncomfortable. He knows this, too.

1

"Then we're going to lose Ondine," he responds, voice quivering.

Zippi-doo-a, zippi-doo-a, ringa ranga rung rung!

In the bar on Ondine, the man orders another dark brown ale and feels his loneliness more acutely here, in the midst of a crowded nightclub, than alone in his hotel room. He wishes wistfully that he'd had a childhood, that he'd learned to dance.

Zippi-doo-a, zippi-doo-a, ringa ranga rung rung!

Aboard the battle cruiser, the admiral discovers that he is out of stomach pills, even though they were a hundred to the bottle. Angrily, he throws the empty bottle at the wall, then stares in frustration at the computer projections of friendly and enemy forces and sees the tremendous bulge in the front. He knows his needs. He needs at least eight, possibly nine cruiser-class vessels to punch that bulge in space back in. Failing that, he needs to get roaring drunk.

Both needs are impossible to fulfill in his present position.

Umi-bobba, umi-bobba, wingi wangi wong wong!

The man in the Ondine bar looks at the girl in the line. She is radiant, alive, lost in the music and the togetherness of the dance. Not attractive, not at all: stringy black hair, jaw overlarge, badly overweight in all the wrong places. But there was a fire in her, an energy, a life-force when she joined in the dance. He downs his ale and wishes longingly to feel that in himself, but inside there is only a hollow emptiness.

Umi-jada! Umi-jada! Wamma wamma bing bang!

The admiral sighs. Without the firepower of the *Dagger* the bulge is enlarging, starting to curve in. It seems so tiny on the great electronic map board, a matter of mere centimeters. Actually, it was less than that when set just against the size of the front, let alone the size of the galaxy. Just a speck among the four-thousand-plus human worlds linked in the defensive unit called the Combine.

Yes, he notes, the sadness welling up in him, the

bulge starts to loop, starts around that tiny little dot there, that one little flyspeck no bigger than a pinhead.

That world, where people were still dancing in joyful ignorance.

Jami-bobba, jami-bobba, rama zama dong dong!

He'd met her only a few hours earlier, looking forlorn and alone on the beach facing the ocean. Her name was—let's see, what was it, now? Azu—Azure Pontine. An interesting name. Kind of a pretty name, really. He'd started up a mild conversation about the sea birds, and she'd responded. That didn't happen often, not to him. She flirted, he made a pass, and they started touring the clubs and carny attractions up and down the beach. It'd been fun. More fun than doing it alone, the way he was used to doing it. And then they'd been passing this joint and she'd heard the bong dance, and that's how it stood.

Umi jama! Umi jamma! Wamma wamma bing bang!

The admiral orders more stomach pills and bawls out a few aides for minor nothings with a fury that surprises even him. They don't mind; they understand. They are feeling the same way themselves, and this has happened to them before. That's why they're on the flagship.

The admiral, they know, is putting off the inevitable as long as possible.

Jami-bobba, jami-bobba, rama rama ring rang!

The man is unsure of his own feelings, and he doesn't like that. He'd always prided himself on his self-control, but the older he got the less able he was to control anything. He was becoming a creature of emotion, dark emotion, and it was eating him alive. He knows this, admits this, but feels trapped. He knows intellectually that he seized upon this girl because she was someone, another human being, someone who was with him despite a total lack of understanding of him, or even a care about him. That, too, was all right; nobody ever cared, nobody ever understood. *He* cared—cared so much that he tortured himself constantly, desperately wishing that he could be a part of them, a part of humanity, and not a thing apart, knowing that something inside of *him* created the wrongness, unable to know what it was or do anything about it.

Lights flicker, the happy line of dancers kicks and reels to the beat of the combo, their shadows flickering against the studded tapestry backdrop of the dance floor; shadows that move and flow as a single organism, joined, linked together visually as in the rhythm of the dance, while the man's shadow does not touch the dance floor, although it reaches for it.

Zippi-doo-a, zippi-doo-a, ringa ranga rung rung!

The admiral pushes back his white hair, which seems greasy and thick to his touch. He realizes for the first time that he is sweating, that he is feeling every ache he ever felt in his life, including aches not so much of the body as of the soul.

He looks around the command bridge and wants to cry, not just for the defeat, not just for the souls on a planet named Ondine, soon to be lost no matter what he does, but for them—these incredible men and women who feel as frustrated, as tired, as angry, and as sick as he, yet perform their own duties as experts. *They* didn't have young, dedicated officers to take it out on. Perhaps they had friends, even relatives, down there. Certainly most of them had visited the beautiful world at one time or another. A perfect shore-leave place.

Who do they take their feelings out on? he wonders idly, feeling suddenly foolish and ashamed. He knows they understand, but that makes it worse, not better. They have nobody to take it out on.

They didn't have his responsibility, either.

Zippi-doo-a, zipp-doo-a, ringa ranga rung rung!

The man takes out a sinkweed and lights it, inhaling deeply. He knows that interaction with the ale will make him high as a kite, but it's all he has. Why was she alone on the beach? he wonders idly. Why did she pick him? Probably because I look safe, he decides. He always looked safe: fat, tall, balding, a trace of a goatee that didn't work on his oily, pitted face. A shy, halting manner; they *knew* he understood. Everybody's big brother.

He hates the dance line. He studies their faces, wonders which one would make a pass at her, take her away from him. The flickering lights seem to mist in front of him, forming an intangible, transparent barrier. *They* are on the other side of the barrier, with her.

Umi-bobba! Umi-bobba! Wingi wangi wong wong!

The circle is closing, forming a larger bulge on the screen.

"Messenger's hit!" comes a call from the ensign. She looks up at the admiral, expectant but with hollow eyes.

He tries to force water to his cracked lips, but feels only bile. Finally, he manages a soft, almost inaudible croak.

"Withdraw and regroup," comes the broken whisper, the deadly ghost of words they cannot prevent or exorcise.

"Aye, sir," comes the slurred reply.

The bridge is silent for a long period, but the order has already been sent, received, and by the flickering of cheap little lights, acknowledged.

Finally the old man, for now he is just that, not an admiral commanding a battle, looks up through tears.

"How many people on Ondine?" he asks. There are no tears left in his eyes, but they pour out of his voice.

"Not many, sir," comes a consoling reply. "Almost unpopulated, really. After all, it was designed as a resort, not a mother planet."

"How many?" he demands in a tone that would have cut cold steel.

The ensign stiffens. "Sixteen million, give or take," she replies crisply, like she was giving the number of tomatoes on Farm Number 34.

"Sixteen million," the old man repeats in wonder. "Only sixteen million?" He stiffens, his face contorted with rage. *"Only* sixteen million?" he roars. "ONLY SIXTEEN MILLION!" He is screaming now.

The bridge seems impossibly large, the people in it mere specks, like the tiny little lights on the war board, like the tiny little dot that is Ondine. The anguish is a living thing, bouncing from wall to wall, corner to corner.

The ship is pulling out, pulling back, but not the people aboard her. Their bodies are going, for certain, but their minds are fixed on Ondine.

Umi-jada! Umi-jada! Wang bong BONG!

The dance is over now. The dancers release each other's hands and struggle to their places. The girl moves toward him, toward the stool next to his, where her boilermaker demands attention now. She is laughing, smiling, and almost flopping onto the stool, she leans back and spins once around.

"Wheeee!" she breathes, chest heaving, and he laughs at her exuberance, as if that laugh for one precious moment makes him a part of it. He lurches slightly, almost falls off his stool, catches himself.

She laughs again—it's a pleasant laugh; she has a soft and sexy voice that doesn't go with her looks at all. She'd be the greatest sex symbol on Ondine if she were on the radio.

"You're tight!" she accuses playfully, then downs her double whiskey and reaches for the ale. "Got a sink-weed?"

He chuckles, gets one, lights it and hands it to her.

"You're flying pretty high yourself," he responds lightly. "And that thing with a boilermaker ain't gonna help any."

She inhales deeply, then chugs some more of the ale. He watches almost admiringly; the three he's had have bloated him.

"Aaah! This is Ondine!" she responds. "Anything goes on Ondine! That's what it's here for!" She finishes the last of the ale. He lights another sinkweed for himself.

Suddenly her head darts up. That playfulness is

still in her voice and manner and in her crooked smile. She reaches over, grabs his arm.

"C'mon! Let's go visit the ocean again!"

She almost pulls him off the stool, and they are running now, out the wide doors of the club, out into the twilight.

The ocean's roar is just across the brick lane inexplicably called a "boardwalk." The lights of the joints and tourist traps seem remote once they reach the beach, now shrouded in dusk, the noise of the clubs, the rides, the attractions, the people all mixing in a wild crescendo with the crashing of the surf and the final call of sea birds warning of the approaching dark.

They are flying, sailing along in a chemically induced elation enhanced by the setting sun and the cooler evening air.

Now they are running, running through the surf, which reaches out gently for them, touches them, splashes them. It feels tingly and they laugh, she still running ungainly, dragging him by the hand she clenches tightly.

Finally she stumbles, and he can't stop, falling on top of her.

She giggles, reaches over to him, pulls him to her. They kiss. They embrace. It's a long, long time, or no time at all.

Finally she relaxes, and so does he, and they lie there on the beach, wet and full of sand, looking out at the darkening horizon.

"The sun's set," he notes for no particular reason except there is nothing else to say.

"But there's an afterglow," she responds. "It's beautiful against the clouds."

He looks hard, watching the deep magenta glow reflecting against Ondine's ever-present cloud cover and the roaring sea, so different in the lighter gravity than seas he'd known, like sheets rippling, twisting the afterglow reflection into a million strange and fiery shapes.

They watch for what seems the longest time, until the afterglow has all but disappeared.

It only lasts a few brief minutes, she thinks. How lucky we were to have caught it.

Now it's the awkward time, he thinks, the growing blackness bringing back the deep emptiness and fear in his own soul. Now what? Do I sit here with her all night? Should I make a move? Will she walk away if I make a move? Oh, God! I don't know what to do, and she seems to be waiting for something. Here it is again!

At first she doesn't sense his unease; then, for a moment, she can't figure it out, and begins to feel let down. Am I this bad? she thinks for the hundredth time. Even here in the dark? Is he thinking of a nice way to drop me like most of them do?

Finally she snuggles up to him; the wind begins to make the wet clothing feel clammy and irritating. He accepts her, puts his arm around her, and she leans into him.

"Do you have a room near here?" she whispers in her best voice.

He nods, excitement rising in him at the question, but wary lest he lose the moment too soon.

"Just up the 'walk. A short walk from here."

"Ocean view?" she asks.

He nods, although it's too dark now to see. "Oh, yes."

He gets up, offers his hand, and she pulls herself to her feet. He puts his arm around her, and they walk to his hotel.

Both feel conspicuous and guilty in the hotel lobby, and both look a mess, but this is nothing new to the hotel personnel, who hardly notice. They board the lift capsule, which is mercifully vacant, and he says "Ten," and the thing shoots up to that floor in eleven seconds.

He is still nervous, still sure this evening must go sour, and he has trouble unlocking the door. Finally it opens, and as they enter the soft lighting comes on.

It is a typical Ondine beachfront room; one wall is transparent, looking out at the ocean but seeing only darkness now; a desk, a small table, a couple of padded chairs, and a huge round bed.

"Can you make the windows so we can feel the sea breeze and hear the ocean?" she almost whispers. "I've got to get the sand off."

He chuckles, and sets the window. The field dissolves, leaving an apparent wall-sized opening into space. The sea breeze and salt smell comes through, and the crashing of the waves mixes with the human circus that will go on until all hours of the night. He feels nervous at this setting, even though he knows that the same energy field that creates the window is still really there, preventing anyone from actually falling out or, as he'd considered more than once, jumping.

There is the rush of a waterspray from the bathroom.

"Turn the lights out completely," she calls from inside. He does, and finds that there's still the faintest light reflected from boardwalk to air.

He undresses himself, the sand irritating him. He senses more than hears her emerge from the bathroom, since the rear of the room is very dark. He goes into the bathroom, wipes himself off, and returns to her.

She is standing in front of the window wall. He can see her, faintly, in the light-glow. She is nude, as is he.

She hears him, and turns slightly. He goes up to her, and puts his arm around her.

Finally, they walk over to the bed. The night air coming in now is slightly chilly, and their skin feels cold to the touch of the other.

He is sex-starved, ravenous. She is mechanical; there is no feeling, it's all take and no give. She is satisfied in a few minutes; he is just getting warmed up. She is not used to this sort of man, and she is puzzled and concerned, feeling guilty, as if she did something wrong. She lets him keep at it, but it's no good, her moment has come and gone, and she slowly, sadly lets him know it.

She apologizes softly, but it is he who feels guilty, and somewhat sad. He will not press. The moments were enough. For a brief time, "I" was "we" and that was more than he'd experienced in a long, long time.

It's *still* "we," he thinks, arm loosely around her. Until tomorrow, anyway. There's another human being with me until tomorrow.

And, for now, that's enough.

At 2640 hours Ondine time the lights on the boardwalk at Lamarine went out for good. They were together, asleep, and did not notice it.

No one shut off the night, or the breeze, or the roaring sea.

Antiphony

GENJI DIMORDA WAS A LITTLE MAN, NOT SO MUCH IN stature as in personality. A tall, very thin, ordinary-looking fellow with a reedy voice and halting manner. Only when performing his duties could he rise above his mousy manner and be a somebody.

Genji was a press agent.

Untalented and unnoticed himself, he sought what recognition and pride he could by basking in the acclaim of others more fortunate than himself. He straddled a reversed chair, contemplating the person who made him something greater than he was.

Moira Sabila had just come in from swimming, or pretending to swim, anyway. All she really did was walk to the pool and attract people like honey attracts flies: tall, perfectly proportioned, with hip-length fiery-red hair and enormous blue eyes. Some people, rich people, paid large sums to have themselves made over to look like Moira, but didn't have to; she was born to it.

"Can I brush your hair?" Genji asked, almost shyly.

She smiled a wicked little smile of extreme satisfaction. She knew the power she commanded over Genji and the legions like him, and she reveled in it even as she had contempt for them. Poor little pitiful grubs like Genji, who never had sex they didn't have to pay for, who walked unnoticed by the thousands along the boardwalk—they existed, she was sure, to pay homage to her.

His touch was gentle, worshipful as it should be, and she enjoyed the expression on his face reflected in her mirror, knowing that, had the image been a picture, no one would have noticed him in it.

Genji himself was a bundle of uncontrolled emotion. He loved her, loved her passionately, and would cheerfully have jumped out the window of the penthouse should she command and the safety devices allow.

She doesn't know what it is to be alone, to be lonely, he thought, more with envy than with bitterness. Even the ugly women, they could get men, get laid when they wanted to.

But not Genji.

He'd thought on it often, this unfairness. The fact that men seemed to need sex and human company more than women—at least the ones he knew. He'd once toyed with the idea of having a sex change, but that wouldn't help. He liked being a man, and he loved women.

But women never liked him. They never seemed to consider Genji's feelings and problems, particularly when, like Moira, they couldn't even comprehend a problem like his.

Being around Moira constantly was torture; he was a piece of furniture to her, a servant who was more thing than person, and every day her coldness and indifference to him inflicted new emotional scars on him.

But she was all he had; more than most have. She was famous; a promo model known to billions on many worlds. She was rich. She was beautiful.

Deep in his mind he dreamed of her becoming one day the greatest personality in the Combine. The salary of a press agent for such a star would more than pay to remake him into Adonis.

"That was a great party at the casino," he said casually to her as he started to massage her neck and shoulders. Actually, it had been a terrible party; he always hated parties. There is nothing so horribly lonely as being in a merrymaking crowd of which you were an observer rather than a participant.

She nodded. "Juda always throws such marvelous affairs. Everybody who was anybody was there. I wish we could have stayed."

He stopped the massage and shrugged. "You know we have to shoot at dawn. This is a big account—Red Star Lines will have your beautiful face and figure on wallscreens on every known planet. And they're shelling out a real bundle for the privilege."

She sighed. "I know, I know. But it's such a *bore.*"

She got up and studied her nude body clinically in the mirror, posing first this way, then that. Genji was almost overcome; he always was, although he knew he'd have to be content as usual with what he was getting.

"Good night, Genji," she said softly, almost kindly, and got into one of the beds.

Slowly he turned, waved his hand over the sensor dropping the light to *Off,* and made his way to his own bed.

"Good night, Moira," was all he could ever manage.

Sten Rolvag downed the last of his whiskey and chomped on his fat cigar. His chunky, muscular body turned in its bar chair to survey the scene, and he absentmindedly wiped a little spilled liquor from his magnificent blond beard.

Tanned, face lined, he needed only a horned helmet to become the image of the legendary Vikings of old Earth. In fact, he was a professional hunting guide, and had been since his retirement from the marines a good ten years before.

He sighed, presented his account card for processing to the little slot before him in the bar. The slot swallowed the card, then popped it halfway back up for him to take back. As with all purchases large and small, the drink was paid for with the little card that allowed the payment machinery to deduct its price from his account.

He glanced at his watch. It was much too late, he realized. The watch read 2513. In just under five hours he was due to lead a small party back into the bush. It might be an interesting group, too, he thought. Four women, going in for some *gar*-fish trophies in the Kouisco Lakes district, and maybe an antelope or two. Six days. Six thousand units, which he could use. And maybe a little wilderness fun.

He'd met them earlier, of course. Neither attractive nor ugly, just ordinary-looking women; an accountant, a lawyer, and two engineers. Typical career people, all from the same company, out to take a break from four walls and office routine. They looked like the type who lived their jobs, he thought. Probably haven't had any fun since last vacation. And probably a little sick of their stuffy, bureaucratic coworkers.

Rolvag knew he appeared to be an eccentric character, somewhat swashbuckling and romantic. He worked hard at that image, and after so long he had it down to a fine art.

The night air of Lamarine went through him, made him more awake than ever.

Damn! he thought in disgust. *I'll never get to sleep tonight. Too much noise, too many lights, too many people.*

He accepted it; Lamarine always affected him this way. It was uncomfortable, oppressive, gaudy. He wouldn't be happy until he was back, back out in the bush, back with the peace of nature.

Or so he told himself.

In all the years of cultivating his romantic image, he had come to believe it himself.

He passed an automated news vendor and noticed the little red light flashing repeatedly, telling all prospective customers that something important had just happened.

He stopped, put his card in the slot, and punched *Printout* instead of *Voicebox*. Printouts were cheaper, but so few people knew how to read, or needed to, these days.

The box whirred, and a paper dropped into a slot below. His card popped back out, and he pocketed it, then reached down and unfolded the surprisingly slim up-to-date edition, printed just for him a few moments before.

He moved over to the light from a nearby amusement ride and squinted at the page.

MACHISTS MOVE ON ONDINE IN SURPRISE ATTACK, the headline read. He frowned, a coldness growing inside him, and read the story.

> *Combine Military Command reported this morning that surprisingly strong Machist forces launched a concentrated attack far outside normal battle lines and sites, at a point near Ondine. Combine Command assured the* Star *that, despite some initial losses due to the surprise and intensity of the attack, units were being rushed in to reinforce the stricken area, and that there was no danger that Ondine would be overrun.*

He looked at the little diagram, and his heart sank. As an old military man, he knew unmitigated bullshit when he read it. Ondine was lightly defended—it was forty light-years behind the lines, had no important resources, no war role, and sparse population, so was hardly a likely area for an attack. And hardly an area the navy would put much in to protect, either, he thought sourly. Particularly since the forty light-years between Ondine and the front contained no habitable planets, nothing at all.

He tossed the paper into a waste-reclamation can and headed for a phone booth a few meters away on the boardwalk. Nervously, he slipped in his account card and spoke a number into the transceiver. There was a click, then a buzz, and he had his connection.

He sweated as the tone continued, continued much longer than it should have.

"C'mon, Fally, be there," he whispered under his breath. "Answer your goddamn phone!"

Finally there was a second click, and a petite soprano voice said, "Shore Patrol, Captain Falsitti's office."

"I need to talk to the captain," Rolvag told her. "Tell him it's Sten Rolvag."

The woman on the other end was apologetic, but also slightly nervous and disoriented. "I'm sorry, sir, but there's nobody here."

"Then give me the duty officer," he told her.

Her voice almost trembled. "Sir, I mean *nobody's* here. I'm just a private. I was on leave, heard the news, and tried to find out what was going on. It's deserted here, sir. There's nobody at all on the base."

Rolvag felt his stomach turn. He knew what the lonely private was just starting to dare think.

Of course the ships would be gone—what dinky little tubs there were, anyway. But not everybody. Not the SP's, the headquarters command. Not the secretaries, and clerks, and phone operators.

Unless . . .

"Private? You still there?" he asked softly, thinking as he spoke.

"Yes, sir?"

"You know of the attack?"

"I—I heard it on the news, yes, sir. But they said they had it contained!" The tone was almost pleading now.

"You know what it means for the base to be evacuated, don't you?" he responded slowly, carefully.

"They can't have evacuated, sir! They just—they just wouldn't leave us here. They evacuated Tramion and Calliande and Sopolene! They wouldn't desert us here on Ondine!"

He sighed. "They had time before. They expected the attacks, and they had the transports ready. Yes, I'm afraid they would evacuate. Check the code room if you doubt it. I'll bet it's a mass of molten metal right now."

For a long while there was silence at the other end, but he could hear her breathing. Finally she wailed, "Sir? What are we going to do now?"

Sten Rolvag chomped on his cigar.

"You stay there. Any other military show up, tell them to stay put with you. You navy or marine?"

"Marine, sir."

"Good, good," he said, almost to himself. "That means you know how to fight. Okay, I'll be there as soon as I can. Round up anything that looks useful for a firefight."

"What are you going to do, sir?" she responded, relieved that someone seemed calm and had a plan.

He considered his reply.

"We're going to do what marines throughout human history have done when left behind. We're gonna go into the bush and continue the fight. What else *can* we do?"

Rolvag disconnected and put his card back into his pocket. He was glad the flyer was filled with supplies; he had lots more at his camp in the bush.

Almost absentmindedly he scanned the skies of Ondine, pitch-black in the deepening night, as if he might see the invaders coming in, right at him.

He wondered how long they had.

He went immediately to his flyer and drove down to the Surf 'N Sands Hotel. He walked into the lobby, went to a house phone, and called his clients.

It was some time before one of them answered, sleepily.

"This is Sten Rolvag," he told her crisply. "Wake the others, get dressed and packed, and be ready to leave quickly. The navy has just evacuated from Ondine, and we're lost to the Machists. We have to move fast."

There was a long pause, then the woman spoke. "Oh, my God!" was all she could manage.

So far there were six, counting himself. He could carry only a few more in the flyer, he knew. He hoped that at least one or two others would have joined the private at SP headquarters.

The four yawning women from Grumett Corporation looked sloppy and unkempt.

And scared to death.

Their luggage, what they would need for the trip, was all packed on the flyer. One carried their toiletries case.

The lawyer looked particularly nervous. "Is it true?" she asked him, hoping for, expecting some cruel joke.

He nodded. "It's true. Let's move!"

They piled into the flyer, stunned and sleepy, and watched him climb in and throttle forward to the north of the city. There was little traffic this time of the morning, and he wasn't paying much attention to the traffic laws anyway.

The four women rode as if in a dream, unable to think, unable to react to this new nightmare in their lives.

Finally, Rolvag pulled into a parking area just beyond a gatehouse and set the flyer to idle. He turned to the four passengers. "Wait here," he ordered. "I'll be back quickly."

The private was still inside. She was a dark, thickly set woman of perhaps eighteen who didn't mirror her petite voice at all. Her name was Amara. She was alone.

"I'm Rolvag," he told her, and she looked at him in surprise.

"I—I thought you were a marine officer," she stammered.

He smiled. "Honey, I was happily retired until tonight, but right now it looks like I'm the commanding general of the whole goddamned Marine Corps. Let's go." He looked around. "Nobody else?"

"A few calls," she responded. "Nobody would believe me. They thought I was supposed to put them on stall because of the combat situation." She looked around. "Nobody came, as you can see."

"Weapons?" he asked her. "Anything usable?"

She shook her head negatively. "No, nothing but my issue sidearm. What they didn't take they blasted.

S.O.P. You should know that. Leave nothing for the enemy."

Rolvag grunted. "I was afraid of that. Well, okay, we'll make do with what we have. Let's go."

She looked at him strangely. "Go? Go where? What good will it do?"

He felt irritation rising within him. "We're going to remain free until they liberate us, and we're gonna make it hot as hell for the Machists. Now, come on!"

She looked around again at the deserted office.

"What are we supposed to do that with?"

"With me," he replied, grabbing her arm and pulling her along. She did not resist.

Obbligato

Observations on worlds conquered by the Machists, particularly Calliande, indicate a deep knowledge of human behavior patterns. The human race was obviously well researched before the start of the war, probably for decades. As a result, we find that they have developed a system for dealing with captive indigenous populations which is at once crude, vicious, and effective. The first stage we call the despair and weeding process, and it parallels much in human history.

For, in order to effectively control and assimilate a hostile population, you must first show the absence of hope.

—A Primer on Machist Behavior,
p. 812, Naval College, 1161 A.C.

HE LOOKED LIKE AN AD FOR A PLAS-PARLOR. MEDIUM height, thin and muscular, with deep brown eyes and carefully shaped, thick, wiry black hair. He looked, in fact, almost *too* perfect: not a scar, mark, mole, or pimple on him.

He glanced around the sterile office dispassionately, as if his mind were somewhere else, pondering more important matters. Inwardly, he chuckled at the place.

It looked like the office of a typical small import-export firm, which was what the door alleged. He had no doubt they actually *did* some business here, but he wondered if anyone interested in knowing what the place really was couldn't find out without much effort.

The receptionist was a mousy little man, the kind with "clerk" stamped all over him—the sort that barely glances up at you, and never looks you straight in the eye.

"I'm here to see Mr. Hudkins," the visitor said in a quiet and expressionless voice. "I have an appointment."

"Well, ah, I see, sir," harumphed the clerk. "And who shall I say is here?"

"Just tell him it's Daniel," the dark man replied. "He'll know who I am. He sent for me."

The clerk reached over and touched a small stud next to his intercom. Instantly a noise blanker cut off all sounds for a few centimeters around the equipment, so that no one could hear what was said.

No ordinary man. Daniel could have neutralized the blanker or read the man's lips, but he didn't. It wasn't worth the trouble.

The clerk touched the stud again. "Ah, go right in, sir. Third door to the right. Has his name on it."

Daniel nodded and walked down the hall to the proper office. He paused, considered knocking, then decided just to barge in.

Admiral Hudkins looked much the way one would expect him to look—tall, thin, a bit stooped, with a fine-lined face and rich handlebar mustache. He stood as Daniel entered, and motioned him to a chair.

Daniel took it, although he had no need of chairs and such. But formalities were part of the act, and they always made the people he dealt with feel better, even when they knew his true nature, as Hudkins did.

The Chief of Naval Intelligence got right to the point. Unlike the clerk, he was direct, brusk, and looked everyone in the eye.

"You've heard about Ondine?" he asked the visitor.

Daniel nodded. "Hell of a mess. How'd you let them slip it past you like that?"

The admiral looked almost apologetic. "We got suckered, that's all. They know we have some people on their captive worlds—they catch one occasionally. They did a big show for us, nice little secret documents, ship orders, and the like. Various ships showed up at various places, supposedly on the way to other places, and the like. The plan was supposed to be a hit at Ariante, with a feint at Ondine. We believed them. Ariante is a tempting prize, only nine light-years from the current front, six billion people, lots of heavy industry. So we adjusted accordingly, and we were suckered. That's what hurts the most about this one— losing a planet is bad enough, but to be suckered out of it . . . well, it's galling."

Daniel shrugged. A sadness, yes, and a humiliation; but that is the nature of war.

"So what does this have to do with me?" he asked in that same soft voice.

The admiral reached down and grabbed some charts, then leaned over and handed them to the other man. "The top chart is the position of the front over a ten-light-year sector on both sides of Ondine as it existed before the attack. Now flip over the first transparency."

Daniel did, and suddenly the line changed. Twenty, thirty enemy ships were shown in picket position around Ondine. The distance of the line was about four light-years.

"Looks like a lock on Ondine to me," Daniel said honestly.

"Go to the second map. That shows dispositions for ten times that first one's distance. Now look at it, with the Machist ships in the same position."

Daniel did so, and saw immediately what the older man meant. Now, instead of a mild bulge, there was a diagonal line almost forty light-years away from Ondine, with a bulge like a soap bubble that hadn't yet come free from its blower-ring. It was long, and sliced through essentially unoccupied space for the full forty light-years plus the four around Ondine.

"They're bringing up ships fast," Hudkins told him, "but there's no way a position like that can be defensible. Not forever."

"Why not just take a big group in and break it?" Daniel asked.

Hudkins looked worried. "We can't. Ships can only be built so fast; people can be trained to man those ships properly only with time to do so. We're already stretched thin. In a couple of years, perhaps as many as five, we'll increase our strength upward of ten times what it is now. Enough, we think, to punch holes in that line wherever we want. But now—the front's moved past the human frontier, back into our front yard. Places like Ariante must be defended to the utmost. Priorities must be set. If we weaken one to retake Ondine, the enemy will hit us there and force further losses."

Daniel nodded slowly. "It does seem a pity, though, that such an obvious weakness can't be exploited."

Hudkins smiled broadly. "Yes, doesn't it? Remember, this thing works both ways. Machist supply lines are stretched dangerously thin. Fighters slip under the front and break that continuity still more. Ondine looks to us like a commander's desperation to win a battle because his superiors are frustrated with stalemate. But, like us, they can't spare the ships and men to fortify it heavily."

"How soon before you think you can take it back?" Daniel asked.

The admiral shrugged. "We'll need a year at least, maybe more if we get any more nasty surprises, or if they unexpectedly try and fortify the place."

Daniel spread his hands. "Then what's the problem? We *are* going to take it back; it's simply a matter of waiting for our time to come."

The intelligence chief frowned. "It's not a question of that—it's a question of what we find when we take it back." He paused, considering his words carefully.

"You see," he continued, wetting his lips nervously, "there's only a small population down there. Easy to work with, to manage. Plenty of space to play around. We think there might be another reason for taking Ondine."

Daniel's eyebrows rose. "Like what?"

"An object lesson," the other replied grimly. "A demoralizer of the first water. Sixteen million people—tourists from just about every world you can think of. Plenty of folks around here have friends, relatives, or acquaintances on Ondine. We've seen what the enemy does to people on the worlds they capture. The more time they have the more effective they are, true, but they'll have to do a rush job here. Everything to convert that world and that population into something else, something horrible and different. Something which, when we *do* liberate it, will terrify everyone in the Combine."

Daniel shook his head slowly from side to side. "I don't see how that's possible."

"The facts have been heavily suppressed," the admiral admitted. "It wouldn't do to have them get out. But—well, when the Machists take a world, they convert it. They change it and the people into something alien, inside and out." He sighed. "In the past we could do nothing. Now we need time to keep the same thing from happening on Ondine. That's where you come in. That's to be your job. Slow them down. Use whatever methods you have to. Make sure their project isn't completed before we get there."

It was Daniel's turn to look grim. "You know I've never actually been in action, don't you? I'm a prototype, the laboratory guinea pig. There's been nothing like me before, and nobody, not even I, know how I will act or can act. And infiltrating a taken world, organizing resistance, slowing down or stopping the Machist takeover for an indeterminate period until you can liberate it—it just may not be possible."

The admiral nodded agreement. "I'm well aware of the impossibility of what we're asking, and, frankly,

I'd rather not send *you* in. We don't know enough. You don't know enough." Suddenly his fist banged down hard on his desk. "But, dammitall, man! We have to *try!*"

Daniel left the office quietly and walked out onto the street. The air was warm, but he barely noticed. He looked at the city—at the broad boulevards, moving walkways, silent minitrams, and gardens hanging from the sides of the gleaming buildings.

But that wasn't the city. Not really. A city wasn't a set of structures; those were mere artifacts. A city was people. He watched them on the eternally crowded walkways, an endless stream rushing in and out of buildings, talking, laughing, sometimes interacting.

It had been a long, long time since he'd been in a city, or anywhere except the Combine R&D asteroids off Altair. A long, long time since he had interacted with any but clinical scientists and cartoon bureaucrats.

He started walking down the avenue, walking with the jostling crowd, looking at their myriad faces reflected in the store windows at base level. A human perpetual-motion machine.

He passed the first test, he knew. Nobody gave him a second glance.

He felt the old longing still within him, that longing for company, companionship, humanity. He thought he'd put that all behind him, but he had not. Looking just like them, acting just like them—feeling just like them. He had never realized what it would mean to cut himself off like this. Not until now, with that faceless mob swirling, walking, talking, pressing around him.

He'd come in straight from the spaceport by taxi-cab—he knew it was really the I-boys keeping watch on him. Some of them still were. He knew them, knew where they were, could even selectively tune in their whispers from amid the roar of the city. It didn't matter.

He frowned. *This* mattered.

Almost absentmindedly, he found himself taking a seat near the street in a sidewalk cafe. He glanced down at the little table, pressed *Menu,* and quickly scanned it. He ordered apple pie and coffee—he'd always liked apple pie. Then he presented his account slip and charged the snack to the Combine.

The pie and coffee arrived on a little robotray less than two minutes later. He took them and looked at them in wonder. He switched to a high olfactory mode, and smelled not only the wonders of the food, but the less obtrusive scents of the city as well. A few bites, though, and he knew this was all wrong. Just part of the act. He knew where the food was going, and what would happen to it, and all sensory impressions stopped the moment he swallowed it.

He sighed and left the remains to be cleaned up.

He boarded a tram for the spaceport and took a seat. The tram wasn't particularly crowded; it was midday, not rush hour.

He suddenly became aware of being stared at, and for a moment thought one of those clumsy tails Hudkins used was following him. Then he realized it was a young woman, a teenager really, dressed informally for the summer's heat in what looked like a hula skirt made of a comfortable artificial fiber, sandals, and, except for a pair of large hooped earrings and a small jewel-ring through her nose, nothing else. She had the build for it, he thought. On some worlds that outfit would be cause for panic, but here on Roncik, in the capital city of Nueva Asuncion, it was ordinary casual attire.

She saw him look at her, and smiled. He returned the smile, and she accepted the gesture as an opening. "I'm sorry for staring," she began, sounding not the least bit sorry, "but I couldn't help notice your face and clothes. You're not a Ronnie."

"No, I'm not," he admitted. "I haven't been from anyplace in a long, long time."

She leaned forward, excitedly. "I just *knew* you were a spacer! Your manner—the way you walked when you got on. What ship?"

"A little one," he responded. "My own ship. Basically automated. I'm the only crew."

"Jesus!" she exclaimed. "Don't you get lonely out there?"

He managed a wan smile. Yes, he thought to himself, the dull ache brought back by the city and extended human contact rushing into him. Yes, lonely isn't the word for it. But aloud he said, "No, it's not particularly bad. You get used to it."

"Wow!" she exclaimed, impressed. "I just can't imagine it. All those other worlds, other people, other cultures." She looked almost ashamed. "I've never been more than a hundred kilometers from Nueva Asuncion." She pronounced it "Nuevashunshun," he noticed, as if it were one bouncy word.

"People are people," he told her. "Different hangups, different dress, religion, or whatever, but people are more alike than you'd believe." Or know, he added to himself. Particularly in the important ways, the ways in which human beings treated one another. He looked around at the few other passengers on the tram. Most ignored or pretended to ignore their conversation. Why had she picked *him,* after all, instead of one of them? He was handsome, dressed differently, and with a look that, here, was exotic.

They talked on a little, and she came over and sat beside him. He knew what she wanted, and he knew what he wanted—and that last surprised him, for he'd felt no such sensations for years, and wasn't supposed to be able to feel them anymore. Hormones and all that, they'd said. Well, though it was true he didn't feel the same, the longing was still there. Then, suddenly, he felt the walls close in on him, the barriers only he knew grew suddenly tangible. He knew she had long passed her stop and was expecting him to take her out on the town or show her his ship or somesuch.

The tram ground to a halt at the spaceport, end of the line. He got up, and she followed. Finally, he turned and faced her, towering somewhat over her slender figure. "I'm sorry, but I've got to leave you here. I'm due back on my ship at once, and it's in orbit. I'll have to shuttle up. But it was really good talking to you."

Disappointment was strong in her face and frustration in her stance and manner, but she smiled and shrugged it off. She stood on tiptoe and kissed him lightly.

"Maybe next time you're here."

His expression was strange and distant. "Sure. Maybe next time," he echoed, and turned and walked off.

The man known as Daniel rode the escalator up to the debarkation area, then walked across the main terminal briskly, entering a door marked RESTRICTED AREA—DO NOT ENTER without pause. The warning on the door was unnecessary; only a very few could open it anyway.

A young man with sandy hair turned away from a complex console. "Hi, Daniel!" he called. "How'd it go?"

He sighed. "Worse than could be expected."

The other man nodded sympathetically. "Well, we knew it might be rough. The important thing is that nobody knew you were anything but a dashing space captain."

Daniel managed a chuckle. Important to whom, Mordi? The navy? Sure. The mission? Sure. But what about Daniel? Did anyone ever think about Daniel? Everybody thinks about himself, he concluded, his depression deepening. Nobody ever gives a damn about the other fellow. Everyone thinks of himself as a unique individual, but everyone else—well, they're all just ciphers.

"You ready?" Mordi called to him. "I have clearance in nine minutes."

Daniel nodded. "Might as well. The material on Ondine going to be beamed up to me?"

"I'll have all that for you before you break orbit." Mordi hesitated for a minute, dropping his jocular air, his face growing serious, concerned. "You sure you want to do this? I mean—you feel you want to?"

Daniel sighed. "Mordi, I've had four years as a laboratory rat in every Combine scientist's maze. I'm sick and tired of it, I'm bored, and, in addition, the only way to prove or disprove the system is in the field."

"Okay, then. Get in."

He walked over to a sliding door, pulled it open, and stepped into a cylindrical capsule. The door closed, and then the cylinder snapped shut. He heard the switches and relays, and nodded to himself. All was ready.

The capsule was form-fitting and airtight. As he waited for lift, the little gages told him the interior of the capsule was now a vacuum.

It didn't matter to Daniel.

The capsule ejected, registered as a freight capsule with no lifeform aboard, and climbed rapidly into the sky.

And the listing was correct. There was no lifeform aboard.

Daniel tracked the capsule, locked onto it, and guided it in. It approached rapidly, then decelerated at a rate that would have killed anything human. Now it floated only meters from an opening in what looked like a golden egg perhaps thirty meters in diameter.

Slowly the capsule eased into the open hole, then locked in, its base almost seamlessly flush with the exterior of the egg.

"Feed me the Ondine stuff, Mordi," Daniel ordered.

He wanted to get his mind off the people, the trams, the apple pie, and the girl.

Ripieno

ONDINE WAS DISCOVERED IN 861 A.C. BY A GOVERN-
ment scout. It wasn't great to look at.

The star was G-class, which was good, and the distance from the star to Ondine, second of seven planets
worth mentioning in the system, was about 135 million
kilometers. Its axial tilt was almost 84 degrees, so it
was warm and had little in the way of seasons.

About 80 percent Terra-size, Ondine's gravity was
lighter but only comfortably so. An active planet, geo-
logically; lots of water and mountain ranges, volcanoes,
and whatnot, even though it had a lot of gasses that
humans could do without, and was an inferno. The
place was solid clouds, really—it was too hot everyplace
for water to condense.

But the planet had potential. The Terraformers had
worked with less, but, they had always had some reason
for undertaking difficult projects. This world was off
the beaten track, had few usable resources, and seemed
destined to sit there until it boiled away or became, in
the millennia, something more interesting.

The scout duly filed his report, named the planet
Ondine after his third daughter, and left.

After a suitable interval, wherein the Combine
looked at it, analyzed it, and decided it wasn't worth
anything to them, Ondine was listed on the Exchange.

The Exchange was where groups with money go. It listed all of the discovered worlds and all the pertinent facts. The brokers had all this information at their fingertips. Any one of them, acting for a client, could put in a one-hundred-unit claim on the place, thus giving it to the client for a period of five standard years. If the claim were challenged, the Combine delightedly held an auction, with the rights going to the highest bidder, since one hundred units was roughly the price of a ream of paper.

Who bought worlds? Big corporations sometimes; occasionally local governments, to handle population or other pressures. Religious and political groups were especially active in this field. If they had any kind of following at all, they could raise the money, develop a world on their model, and "prove" their ideas.

And get out of everybody's hair.

The owner could do anything with his planet for the five years, even blow it up, but if he did *nothing,* then it reverted to the listing. Many did.

Ondine had been claimed eleven times in the century following its discovery, but no one could do anything with it. The trouble was cost—nobody had the kind of money it would take to make Ondine livable.

Until Bartol Alvarez Chu Lin came along.

Lin was the kind of man who'd grown rich by exploiting the lives and property of everyone he touched and then felt guilty about it as he grew older. He was upset. He had nine hundred and thirty-eight great-grandchildren and they were living packed into sardine-can cities on nameless worlds, looking for places to play.

Lin had built amusement parks before, but suddenly he dreamed of a new kind—a world that would be the ultimate getaway spot.

Ondine only cost him a hundred units to obtain, but it cost half his fortune to remake the way he wanted it and dreamed of it, money enough to finance several planetary budgets for many years.

The planetary engineers accepted the challenge. They

increased the axial tilt to a perfect ninety degrees, eliminating seasons and stirring up a lot of new volcanic activity which they controlled. They used molten magma to build their land masses, then stabilized the volcanoes. They added a series of inert gasses and applied electrical charges to build and control an upper-atmosphere protective layer around the planet.

The surface cooled—very slowly at first, but it cooled, and condensation occurred. It rained everywhere on the planet. It rained for twenty-seven years, torrentially, while the engineers paid attention to other details.

And once finished, they had a pretty little world, all blue under the ever-present white clouds. Four continental land masses, not huge but large enough, centered in the temperate zones between twenty and seventy degrees latitude. Millions of islands dotting the seas, from a few kilometers square to a few thousand. Some minor adjustments for the proper radiation, heat level, and the like, and they were ready.

Any known lifeform could live there.

In came the Life Boys, as they were jokingly called in the trade. They had clonable tissue from just about every plant and animal that had ever lived in the known galaxy, and samples of almost every microorganism, virus, and whatnot, including ones you'd rather not have.

It was a miniature, high-speed Creation. First the microbes, and when they lived and adapted well to Ondine without producing crazy mutations, more ambitious material was introduced. Simple one-celled animals in the seas, which fed on the microbes. And, of course, plants. Lots and lots of trees atop ground igneous rock that always had made the best soil. The forests would control erosion and add the proper balance. They also absorbed excess water and carbon dioxide.

Ondine became a water world and a jungle. With few natural enemies, the trees and other plants had a field day. Grasses, flowers, all were added in climato-logically perfect areas, even the islands.

The seas were stocked with fish, shellfish, and, eventually, marine mammals in perfect proportion. Food chains were laboriously worked out for sea and land.

Seventy-three years after Bartol Lin claimed the place, Ondine was a wilderness paradise, teeming with life.

Lin himself supervised the final stages. Sixteen strategically placed cities were to be sparkling resorts, places where any kind of pleasure could be found—for a price. The Lin Corporation controlled everything. The gambling was guaranteed honest; justice was swift for those who disobeyed. Sex? Any kind, your perfect match guaranteed. Want to hunt a lion? Fine. Catch king sturgeon in a mountain lake? Great. The sixteen resorts could accommodate you whatever your dreams or desires.

For a price, of course.

And it paid. Oh, how it paid. It was the regular shore-leave port of call for just about everybody's service. It was *the* place to go, the *only* place to go.

Lin even let the Groupies in.

They were called that because they were generally reflections of larger types of groups in society—disaffecteds, political, religious, or otherwise—whose followings, unlike those of the giants, were quite small. They made convenient villagers in the interior, tiny pockets of humanity that could live their own way—as long as they didn't foul up their surroundings—and, incidentally, provide human eyes and ears for the remote spots at no cost to Lin.

Nine million people, eventually, looking after the needs of an estimated six to twelve million tourists, year-round.

Lin retired there, in a way, living like a monarch and being treated like one. He died there, too, when he forgot to strap himself into the deck chair from which he was fishing on his yacht. He hooked one too big for him, was pulled over, and drowned.

But the corporation lived on, and Ondine lived. The dream lived.

Until the Machists attacked.

Man had discovered a few intelligent, nonhuman species as he spread, but most were too different to have much to offer, and they were all planetbound, primitive by human standards.

And then one day, a scout named Creedy discovered a world that was different. Populated by nonhuman land mammals that resembled giant raccoons. They had cities, factories, agriculture—and spaceports.

Creedy never returned. He had reached the edge of another expanding culture, the Machists; and he was absorbed, or destroyed, or whatever.

It was decades before anybody else learned of the other empire. When word came, it was the Machists—they named themselves—with the story of Creedy and an offer to join their empire, which, they said, was made up of tens of thousands of different races all united in a single culture. It was their aim to spread this culture as far as possible, as long as possible, uniting all intelligent creatures in a common union.

The Combine, never well organized to begin with, debated, hemmed, hawed, and finally sent out word that they welcomed contact, trade, and a mutual exchange of ideas.

This announcement seemed to upset the Machists. They hadn't, as it turned out, issued an invitation to humanity.

They had issued an ultimatum.

And they were strong, hard, and tough. They had done such things before, it was clear. Humanity needed the quick loss of only three worlds to unite against the common threat, but much, much longer to learn how to fight an interstellar war.

The Machists gobbled up world after world. Finally, enough strength and experience had been gained by humanity to enable it to dig in and fight. The Machist empire was indeed huge, and the human worlds relatively compact at about a million cubic light-years.

They held, and for some time the front had been stable, each side parrying and thrusting along it but unable to broaden its base.

Stalemate.

And now, thirteen years after the last Machist conquest, they had taken Ondine. It was a small prize, perhaps; a poor prize for such an expanding culture. But it was theirs now, and it had been man's.

Naval Command fretted, and fumed, and puzzled, and wondered why they had picked Ondine, and what motives lay behind their steadfast determination to hold an untenable military position as long as possible.

One thing everyone was certain of: the Machists weren't fools. They never did anything without a reason. They'd been at this sort of thing for centuries, certainly, perhaps for millennia.

The only thing everybody knew was that humanity, now geared entirely to a war footing, was building up its forces at a fantastic rate. Time was on the side of the defenders.

It was assumed the Machists knew this, too.

What did they expect to gain from Ondine?

Piangendo

THE PHONE BUZZED. GENJI DiMORDA HEARD IT FIRST as a ghostly, far-off thing, and it was some time before he realized that it was a real sound with some relevance to him.

I ought to ignore it, he told himself. Probably some schmuck with romantic dreams of Moira.

The buzzing persisted, and he finally bowed to its demand. He knew Moira would never get it; not only did she sleep with blinders and earplugs, but it would have been beneath her to answer her own phone, anyway.

He groped for the instrument on the bedside table and punched its glowing, dull-red button.

"Yeah?" he snapped.

"Mr. DiMorda—this is the hotel security service," the caller began, and suddenly he was wide awake. Thoughts of injury, burglary, everything he could imagine washed through his mind. He sat up, switched the light on hurriedly, and was relieved to see Moira still asleep in her bed and the room apparently undisturbed.

"What's the matter?" he asked nervously.

"We've just been informed that Ondine was attacked and captured by the Machists," the security agent told him. "Everyone is confined to his hotel or dwelling until further notice."

36

The news didn't sink in, not right at the start. He'd never followed the war, or politics, or anything like that. Such things were so far away and so unimportant. He took refuge in the familiar.

"Look, buddy, I don't give a damn about politics. We're supposed to shoot a commercial at dawn."

The voice sounded disgusted and more than a little tired.

"Mr. DiMorda, there is no more commercial. There is no contact with anybody anymore. Mr. DiMorda, we're trapped on Ondine, which is about to be occupied by an alien race that can do any damn thing it wants with us. We're prisoners, Mr. DiMorda. All of us."

There was a click and the line went dead. The security man didn't really care how they took the news. He had three hundred eighty rooms to call.

Genji sat on the edge of his bed, unable to move. At first he didn't know what to do, then his mind clicked and he dialed the spaceport. There were several long rings, then a click.

"Listen, I need two tick—" he managed before an automated voice cut him off.

"I'm sorry, but the spaceport in Lamarine and all spaceports and planetary public transportation centers are closed until further notice," it said. "Please do not move from your current home or hotel."

He sat back down on the bed, bouncing inanely.

"Jesus!" he said, over and over.

The phone rang in a room several stories below. A man stirred, suddenly discovering that his right arm was almost numb. The girl had been resting on it.

Grimacing in pain, he freed himself from her and reached over, punched the button on the phone.

As this was his two hundred and fourteenth call, the security man was by now painfully aware of the difficulty of his simple duty. "Sir," he began, "Ondine has been taken over by the Machists. They are currently occupying this and all other cities on the planet, and they have ordered me to call everyone in the hotel and tell them to stay put until further notice."

Fear gripped him suddenly. "It's not possible!" he protested. "The navy—"

"Is gone, sir," completed the weary caller. "Everybody's gone but the people. Excuse me, I have more calls to make."

There was a click, and everything went dead.

He sat, half erect, thinking of the call and its consequences. Ondine! Of all places, Ondine! And him! In the middle of it!

The girl turned slowly on one side, reminding him that, for once, he was not alone.

He looked at her in the near-darkness, noting that what little light there was came not from boardwalk reflections but from false dawn.

He shook her lightly. At first she didn't stir. He shook her again, a little harder this time.

"Wake up!" he said sharply. "C'mon! Please wake up!"

She stirred, wiped her eyes, opened them a trifle. "What's the matter?" she grumped.

"The hotel—they just called. They said the Machists have captured Ondine and we're all prisoners!"

She yawned strongly. "That's interesting," she managed, and started to go back to sleep again.

He fumed, but did nothing for a moment. Then he got up, suddenly, and turned the lights up slightly, enough to see the keyboard near the bed. He punched *VID* and watched the wall that had been so transparent and open to the sea suddenly flicker and change.

There was a scene, kind of fuzzy, of the spaceport area and the main roads out of it. The streets were crowded with traffic, mostly heading away. The area was brightly lit, and, in the background, several huge, squat ships sat like great golden cockroaches. They weren't anything like the ships he knew; they were alien. Machist ships.

". . . this perch is all we have managed so far," a voice was saying excitedly. "There seem to be a large number of troop transports rolling, and we can see some Ondine trucks and busses being pulled up, but nothing else. Back to you, Rolfe."

The scene shifted to two bleary-eyed correspondents. One, a distinguished-looking man with a bald head and goatee, looked out at the televisor.

"And that's it so far from our rooftop perch," he concluded, then shifted manner and position.

"Repeating what has happened, at about 17:30 yesterday the Machists launched a surprise attack in full force for Ondine, catching the navy totally unprepared. The battle ended about two hours ago, with the crippling of our main defense ships. The navy had no choice but to destroy its supplies here and evacuate what it could before it was cut off. Since that time we have been receiving instructions from the Machists that everyone is to stay where they are, no matter where they are, or be subject to immediate execution. We repeat, they say they will kill anyone attempting to move in the city, and we already know of dozens of incidents where this has occurred.

"About an hour ago four giant transport ships of the Machist fleet put down at the spaceport and began unloading what appears to be troops. We understand from our offices in the other cities that the same thing is also taking place at Ondine's four other spaceports. Machist troops are fanning out all over the city . . ."

What do they look like, I wonder? the man mused. They were supposed to be multiracial. What strange forms were advancing in those dark trucks?

The noise from the televisor finally woke the girl, and she sat up, uncomfortably rubbing her eyes.

"What the hell?" she managed.

"I told you," he responded, still watching the 'visor, which had shifted back to the rooftop view. "The Machists took over Ondine last night while we slept. The navy's gone, beat it out of here. Those are the Machists you see there, occupying the city."

She saw, and shivered at the endless stream of forms moving along the boulevards. The scene had an unreal quality, like watching a movie. She shivered again, then asked quietly, "What will they do to us?"

He shrugged. "Who knows?"

She looked again at the military procession on the screen.

"*They* sure as hell do," she said quietly.

Sten Rolvag picked up his transceiver, noting that he'd cleared the mountains now.

"Sten to Kiley, Sten to Kiley. You there, Kile?"

There was a crackle, and then a faint voice said, "Go ahead, Sten."

"You heard the news?" he asked gruffly.

"About the Machists, you mean? Yeah, I been on the damn network all night alertin' folks," came the thin, reedy voice of the emergency monitor for the mountains district.

"Tell everybody you can to take whatever they can and set up bush camps," Rolvag told him crisply. "They'll have the locations of the base camps from company records in a matter of hours. They're already down, you know."

"Oh, shit," came the response. "You think that's really necessary?"

"You goddamn better well believe it is," the ex-marine replied emphatically. "We don't know what they do to people when they catch them, but I *do* know they round everybody up and march 'em out of the cities and set up c-camps. You tell everybody that before they jam you. Tell 'em no fires, nothin' that'll give 'em away. As soon as we can we'll try and get in contact with everybody in the area and talk over what to do. Right now, the name of the game is not to get caught."

The man at the other end gave a low whistle. "Okay, Sten, I'll get on it. My God! Who'd ever have thought this would happen *here?*"

"Yeah, I know," Rolvag sympathized. "Look, they're probably monitoring right now, so I won't say where

I'm goin'. Just remember the Hurley Mama's. You beat it there when you're through. Okay?"

"Hurley Mama's, right," the comm repeated. Then he added, "Good luck and God be with ya, Sten."

"You too, Kiley," Rolvag responded, suddenly feeling empty. He switched off.

"What's that about Hurley Mama?" the marine asked in her little girl's voice.

"Oh, some time back Edun Ferricks, another guide, had this big, fat couple named Hurley out in the bush. Well, there they are, these two hippos and Edun, and suddenly the Hurley woman goes into yelling about pain and all that stuff. There were some caves nearby so Edun and Mr. Hurley, they get her into one just before the fat woman gives birth to twins! And she was so damned fat she didn't even know she was pregnant!"

Nobody laughed at the story, not even Rolvag.

"So that's where we're going? To those caves?" one of the women asked.

He nodded. "Yeah. Good protection, good ventilation, lots of wild fruit trees, and a good game area," he told them. "And if you know the caves you got a lot of escape routes. Best place to hide out ever invented."

"Is this all really necessary, Mr. Rolvag, or is it just your yen for heroics," one of the engineers asked derisively. "Hiding out in caves! Really! I'm sure facing the Machists would be better than that. After all, we're civilians."

Sten Rolvag snorted. "Ain't no civilians in a war, woman. Listen, what do you think they started the war over? Property rights? Hell, they got more space than we have, more resources. No, they said they were gonna give us their culture. Culture means people, lady. They don't want Ondine, they want the *people* on Ondine. That's what all this is about. *Us.* They want us to do somethin' to us. We don't know what, but wouldn't you rather be uncomfortable for a while until you know what it is they do to us before you rush down to join 'em?"

The engineer opened her mouth to protest, but closed it again.

"By midday, the people like us in the bush might be the only free human beings left on the planet," Rolvag said crisply.

"We will continue broadcasting as long as possible," the newsman announced, looking as if he'd been through hell. "Machist troops are all over the city and, in fact, all over Ondine. I can't imagine why they've allowed us to remain on the air this long."

The man and the girl had sat stunned through most of the night, watching the unchanging panorama, talking very little, absorbed not so much by the drama on the screen as by their own position in the new scheme of things.

Finally, he turned to her and asked, "Do you have any family?"

She smiled bitterly and shook her head. "No, nobody. That's why I came to Ondine. I've been here four years, bumming around, taking odd jobs here and there, existing." She paused for a minute. "What about you?"

He shrugged. "Some old friends and business associates. My family's all dead. Oh, I'll be missed for a while, but it won't cause any dent in things. Nothing that ever happened to me ever did."

Suddenly they heard distant explosions, which, while not nearby, still sent shock waves through the hotel.

"My God!" she reacted, as much in puzzlement as in fear. "What's that?"

There was a second explosion series.

"The screen's gone blank," he noted. "Looks like they finally pulled the plug."

"Can't we find out what's going on?" she asked apprehensively.

He looked at the control panel for the window. "Yeah, here. We can swing it for a city view. Won't be as good as the 'visor boys, but it might tell us something." He punched the code.

The screen flickered, then the city appeared. It took two or three tries for him to locate the distant spaceport, which was much smaller than in the 'visor, but still easy to make out.

"The ships!" she exclaimed. "The ships are gone!"

That was true. There wasn't a trace of activity in the spaceport, nor signs of massive traffic.

He was just about to reply when another explosion went off, this time visible to them. A few seconds later, the hotel shook again.

"Oh, my God!" she breathed. "They're blowing up the spaceport!"

Explosions came in more rapid succession, and they could see huge billows of smoke and debris roar out of the spaceport. Towers collapsed, supports collapsed, then were obscured in great clouds of dust and dirt rising upward into the sky. It was past dawn now.

"Why would they do that?" she asked him, almost in shock.

He thought of several reasons. "Now that they've unloaded, they don't want anybody else coming in or going out. They probably will blow all of them except one, the better to control who goes in and out of Ondine."

"But that means we're trapped!" she responded, appalled.

The shock waves of the explosions awakened Moira Sabila. She twisted and moaned, then unplugged her ears and flipped the blinders up, a puzzled expression on her face. She looked over at the other bed and noted that Genji was gone. As a more dramatic series of explosions went through the hotel, shaking everything that wasn't nailed down, she felt momentary panic.

"Genji!" she almost screamed. "Genji! What the hell is going on?"

He heard her and came back into the bedroom. He was dressed, but looked as if he hadn't slept a wink. His expression was grave.

"Genji! Thank God!" she managed. Her relief at

seeing him gave him a sense of satisfaction and a slight thrill. *She* needed *him* now.

"The Machists attacked Ondine and captured it last night," he told her. "We're under an army of occupation now."

Color drained from her, and she was wide awake. "Good lord! Why didn't you wake me?"

He turned his palms up. "What was the use? We're confined to the hotel until further notice anyway. One of us might as well sleep."

Suddenly her mind buzzed with all the things he'd already been through.

"Call the spaceport! Let's get out of here!" she urged him.

"Did it," he replied crisply. "No go. There are no spaceships anymore. They all scrammed. And those explosions you're hearing—they're blowing up the 'port. They're trapping us here but good."

"But we have money, dammit all!" she protested. "Genji! Fix it up! Any price to get us out!"

He shook his head sadly. He wasn't much brighter than average, but he'd been getting quite an education in the past few hours.

"Honey, money's no good for anything anymore. Our assets are on Tinderman, anyway, and there's a lot of big, bad battleships between here and there."

"The jewels!" she exclaimed, suddenly brightening. "They're worth something!"

"Nothing," he replied, voice hollow. "Nothing's worth anything anymore, babe."

She got up and went to her dressing table. Ordinarily, lust at the sight would have overcome him, but, right now, it just didn't seem to matter. Nothing mattered anymore.

"What're you doing?" he asked her, almost absently.

"Dressing," she replied, an undertone of arrogant confidence still in her voice. "Soldiers are soldiers and I was never very political, anyway."

He sighed and sat back on the bed as the hotel continued to vibrate from the explosions. His biggest fear at that moment was that she was right—and where did that leave him?

Several floors below the man and the woman were still in bed. There was nothing else to do and nowhere else to go.

From down the hall came the sound of three strong knocks. She trembled with fear, and he held her to him, hoping that he could comfort her, hoping that she didn't realize that he was trembling, too.

A minute or so later the knocks were repeated, a wee bit closer now. They both knew what it was. It was fate, coming slowly, methodically to them.

In a few minutes, it was close enough for them to hear a door slide open, hear muffled voices without being able to make out words. Whoever it was, was coming down the hall toward them.

Finally they both stared across the room at their own door. They couldn't take their eyes from it; although solid and mute, it held them captive.

Then, suddenly, those three powerful knocks were on *their* door, the sound piercing their bodies like funeral gongs.

For a minute he could do nothing. The three knocks were repeated, nastier, more insistent this time. His mind made the door quake with their demand.

"Who is it?" he called out timidly.

No reply. He got out of bed and started toward the door. Suddenly he realized they were both nude, and he grabbed a hotel blanket, wrapping it around him like a skirt. He almost made it to the door before there was a crackling sound, and the locking mechanism barely missed him as it flew halfway across the room before landing on the floor. They had shot the lock off.

It was an old-style door, the kind that opened on hinges. Someone gave it a nasty kick. The door flew back, revealing a sinister-looking little character with a nasty expression. The Machist had kicked the door so hard that it struck the wall and rebounded back as (he? she? it?) stepped in, almost smacking the soldier in the face. If the expression weren't so chilling, it would have been comic.

The Machist angrily pushed the door back open and stepped inside. The girl, still in bed, pulled the sheet up to cover her nakedness and stared in fascinated horror at the strange intruder.

He was about 160 centimeters tall—shorter by a bit than the man, but slightly taller than the girl. He bulged muscle everywhere, like the men in the body-building competitions. Short-cropped curly black hair framed a dark-complected face, and he seemed to have no blemishes on him of any kind. His uniform, made of a light form-fitting material and ending in boots of slightly more substantial stuff, was all black and seemed of one piece.

His eyes were what set him completely apart: yellow rather than white set off huge brown pupils. They looked like a reptile's eyes.

In his right hand he carried a strange-looking contraption that was nonetheless clearly a hand weapon.

He strode into the room arrogantly, looked around it suspiciously, then decided that the occupants were just frightened, not laying a trap. "You will meet in the lobby of this hotel at exactly ten hundred hours— that is about one hour from now," he said in a strange voice, one that seemed to have both male and female characteristics despite the fact that it was totally devoid of emotion. "You will be there and on time. At ten-fifteen the elevators and stairs will be sealed. At ten-thirty this hotel will be gassed, along with anyone still in it." He turned and left. They heard knocking on the room next door.

The man closed the door as best he could and went back to the girl. Her expression, terrified and shocked, mirrored his own.

"I think we'd better get dressed," he said quietly.

Moira was dressed fit to kill. Genji had to admit that. When the insistent knock came to their door, she put on her best smile and pressed the stud that slid back the panels.

A different soldier stood there, but, for all appearances, he was the identical twin of the one downstairs.

Moira gasped, then recovered. There was something strange, uncannily unhuman about the soldier. She forced a smile.

"Won't you come in?" she said pleasantly.

The Machist didn't even give her a glance.

"Any more people in here?" he asked in that strange, machinelike voice.

"Yes, me," Genji called, and came over to the door.

"You will be down in the lobby at ten hundred hours," the Machist soldier began, outlining the same cold threat that most others in the hotel had already heard. He turned and walked off.

"Oh, my God!" he heard Moira whisper. "They're not *people!*"

It took most of the day for Sten Rolvag to make it back to the Hurley Mama's caves after ditching the flyer, whose power-plant radiation could have betrayed them. He had stripped all the camps he knew and his own house for everything he could find—food, weapons, everything. As he approached the caves, he saw Amara sitting on a rock with a hunting rifle in her lap. She froze as he approached, then relaxed when she saw who it was. Gonna have to get some sort of password system, he growled to himself. Wouldn't do to blow each other's fool heads off.

He waved and climbed up to the cave mouth.

"How are things?" he asked.

"Better," she acknowledged. "The little comm radio's still working, and some of the reports are pretty grim. That's made the others a little less complaining."

His expression turned serious. "What's the news?"

"They blew the spaceport at Lamarine completely after unloading thousands of nasty semihuman troops and a lot of equipment. The people have been rounded up and now are crowded on the beaches and in the parks and streets while the Machists gas most of the tall buildings."

"Any resistance?" he asked, mind racing.

"Some," she responded. "They've shot a lot of people. One report said there was a drainage ditch just filled with people's bodies—some dead, some bleeding to death—and that the aliens were covering them over with bulldozers."

He sat alongside her and breathed a long sigh. Until this moment, it'd been old times, fun and games—Sgt. Rolvag to the rescue. Now, for the first time, the enormity of the event was hitting him. Suddenly, the sadness at what was happening was rushing full-force into his mind, as was the impossibility of what he intended to do from here. He looked around at the cave.

Sgt. Rolvag and his Amazon Guerrillas, he thought sourly.

He got up, walked into the cave. He was stunned.

The women had used rugs from his cabin to line and insulate the place. It had a floor, and walls, and looked comfortable. The camp stuff was laid out, cook gear to the rear right now, some oil lamps glowing, folding chairs up and arranged nicely around a little card table, and the sleeping bags and air mattresses laid out in back. Food and ammo and other supplies were neatly stacked far back in the cave.

One of the women brought a cup of what proved to be tea from the little stove and handed it to him proudly. He sipped at it, and it felt good going down.

He noted that there were only three sleeping bags—all the big kind, of course. His always was superlarge because he liked the room, but he was interested in the others. Normally everybody had one of his own, bought in one of the camper stores in Lamarine. This development was not only curious, it took his mind off the marine's report, and as he looked at his motley crew he thought it might not be so bad after all.

"How come the double bags?" he asked the one who gave him the tea. "They cost more than single ones."

She smiled wanly. "This is our honeymoon trip," she explained. "We were all married yesterday. All four of us—to each other."

Rolvag's heart sank.

Vorspiel

DANIEL WAS BORN ON A SMALL, CROWDED PLANET called Diedrian—an old planet, worn and limping, whose denizens were mostly poor and directionless, and usually died young. There were few ways out of there, ever, and these only for the exceptional person.

Daniel wasn't thought exceptional, but he took an avenue that helped. He volunteered for the navy near the beginning of the war, and he let the navy teach him the basic skills, reading and math, and give him the libraries that were his opening to a wider world. He was a good sailor, exceptional for his diligence and dedication, and he had a lot of help in getting the peripheral education needed to pass the entrance tests for the Applied Naval Institute. At thirty-four, he was its oldest student, but the late start didn't deter him. In three years he had his engineering degree for naval rating, and a year after that he qualified as a fighter pilot with the rank—mostly because of his age—of lieutenant.

The fighter was an old human concept but not one used by the Machists. At first the enemy couldn't even figure out what the lightning-fast tiny blips were supposed to signify. They learned fast, as the fighters, racing in well behind the front, hit freighters and supply vessels while avoiding direct combat with larger craft.

The Machists were slow to adapt to change. The fighters chopped them up in the vital-supply-line area until they managed to adjust their tactics. Finally, they started to nail a large percentage of the fighters, even though many continued to break through. Curiously, the Machists never built or bought up fighters of their own.

It wouldn't have mattered much if they had, not really. *They* were the ones with the long supply lines and huge empty spaces; to humanity Machist fighters would have been annoying, but not crippling.

Each fighter pilot had to fly three hundred missions; then he'd be transferred to a bridge subcommand on one of the big ships that was his mother and his base, and that he might, if good there, eventually command.

By Daniel's hundred and ninety-seventh mission, the Machists had gotten good enough to nail one in four fighters per mission. Sixteen or seventeen percent of the fighter pilots lived through the full three hundred.

For Daniel, number one hundred ninety-seven was the end. It was a simple mission, the kind he'd made dozens of times—a large convoy of military supply ships moving from deep in the Machist rear to resupply picket ships along his sector of the front. Twelve fighters set out from the big battleship on the human side of the zone and had little trouble punching some big holes in the enemy freighters.

It had been a simple mistake, really; the pilots call it "zigging when you should have zagged." He swooped in and stuck several torpedoes amidships of a large freighter, then pulled up to miss the exploding target. A huge piece of metal from a different target slightly above him and to the right slammed into his ship.

He woke up, sort of, in what the meds called a brain tank.

Fighter pilots were almost literally wedded to their ships; when the crunch came, much of Daniel's body was crunched and squeezed beyond recognition, but the biomonitoring network continued to provide both a blood substitute and oxygen to the brain. Of course, the shock to his nervous system was such that he was completely unaware of any of this; but the net result was that his brain and spinal column remained intact and functioning, while the rest of him was a mess.

It was rare, almost unheard of, for such a thing to happen. Usually there was some serious or severe break, but in this case there had been none.

Realizing their luck, ambitious surgeons preserved him. They sent what remained of his body back for the regulation hero's burial, but the important part of him went carefully to Naval R&D Labs. They worked on the problem, came up with some connections that would allow him to be brought to full consciousness for a short time, with message input and output. It took a while to overcome the shock, the isolation, but the surgeons were very careful and kept his consciousness highly sedated except for the key periods.

Then they put the alternatives to him, carefully. They could clone another Daniel, yes, but that clone would have its own brain and such. Transplants *were* possible, but they never got one hundred percent of the connections right—the procedure was too complicated; the time they needed for connecting everything exceeded the amount of time they could handle the brain outside of its artificial life-support system. The effects were never the same—cerebral palsy to one degree or another, loss of all feeling and sensation. Nobody was ever really right after it.

He could choose to die, of course. They would permit that, although with great reluctance. This one-in-a-million freak might not happen again.

Or they could make him into a cyborg, a robot with a human brain. But cyborgs never worked well, either. The living part needed too much in the way of life-support to be practical.

However, R&D had a dream looking for a likely subject, and it was that dream that Daniel became. He was wedded to a master computer and life-support combination housed in a golden egg about twenty meters around, with a propulsion system much like that of a fighter but with far greater range. For local service he could put himself in orbit and spread great solar wings for power.

Daniel *became* a spaceship, and the computer increased by a million-fold his ability to handle complex problems.

But what of the ground? What of renewing supplies when they ran low? He needed oxygen and chemical nutrients, even though he had a ten-year capacity within the egg.

Besides, the navy wanted more than a thinking fighter. Civilization had robots by the ton; they did almost all the really tough manual labor, which is why so many people were idle. But even the most complex computer of the self-aware variety could make such robots do only so much.

Daniel was different. The robots the medics and engineers built was undeniably their finest creation. Powered by an energy-beam connection to the spaceship *Daniel,* with a lot of practice it could walk, talk, act, and react, much as the flesh-and-blood original would have. Small relays that he could place in orbit allowed him to be on the other side of a planet and still maintain contact.

The robot was his eyes, ears, and even, thanks to special circuits, nose. He got so he could run the thing so naturally that just about no one could tell it wasn't human. A flesh-form chamber enabled Daniel to design the thing to look any way he wanted, down to the flexible blue veins in his hands and the tiniest hairs on his chest. He could be old or young, male or female. Of course each incarnation had to be 180 centimeters tall and of minimum build. The basic robot inside could not be altered.

Happy with the one, the scientists now got bolder. Additional programing, additional work, and they added another body along with the capacity to run both at once. Without the machine, the human brain could not have done it.

Enraptured by their success, the techs decided to find out how many of these complex mechanisms he could handle at once. With additional computer work, the answer turned out to be twenty-two.

Although trapped forever in a golden egg, Daniel could actually be twenty-two different people at once.

In eleven years of tests and probes and new ideas, the scientists found out everything they wanted to know about their new creations. No less than thirteen thousand people had worked on parts of him at one time or another, most without knowing exactly what they were doing it for, and the most self-aware computers and best human minds in science had poured themselves into him.

The perfect mechanism, the absolute marriage of man and self-aware computer. They'd done it. They were excited. Perhaps this was the harbinger of a whole new group of beings that could go where no one else could, do things no one else could—a device that perhaps, with additional refinement, would make human forces obsolete, carry the war to the enemy, be the shock troops of retribution.

Yes, the scientists, technicians, and government leaders told themselves, they had done it. They'd thought of everything.

It was so like scientists. They never liked things that couldn't be quantified, so they didn't think about them.

It was so like governments, used to thinking of people only as statistics.

It was so like the military, so used to thinking of people as toy soldiers to be pushed around computer maps; congratulating themselves that *only* a few thousand people were lost in a battle.

It was so like them all to forget that somewhere inside that golden egg was a human being.

Lamentoso

After blowing up the spaceport and some large buildings to demonstrate dramatically to the people their isolation, there comes the period of the long march when the population is forced at gunpoint to the countryside. This induces the feeling of being both a prisoner and a property, and secondarily, weeds out the exceptionally frail and rebellious, who are eliminated as object lessons to the rest. Pushed almost beyond endurance, the inhabitants are then split into groups whose size depends on the number of people and the enemy's ability to supply and contain them, and placed in the ultimate degradation situation which we term "denial of technology." Here, despair leads to multiple suicides; the rest, those who cling to hope, can then be rebuilt.

—*A Primer on Machist Behavior,*
p. 962, NC 1161 A.C.

THEY HAD BEEN WALKING, IT SEEMED, FOREVER. THEY were one of many lines of marchers who set out from the city in different directions, but it still seemed as if their own group stretched forward and back forever. Up and down the line were ratlike soldiers of the Machist Army, all of whom seemed identical in every detail, as if they'd all been produced in a factory on the same machine or were all cloned from a single specimen. They spoke little to one another and not at all to the marchers, except to urge them on, prod them, or warn them against conversation.

That was the hardest part. The no-talking rule.

Occasionally people would drop, or protest they could go no farther. They were usually given some chance to go on, to get up and continue. But if they did not, or weren't helped, the soldiers showed no reluctance to vaporize them right there.

Young children and the elderly had been weeded out already. Many parents had been killed protesting; many others, trying to protect their parents, met the same fate.

Night fell, and still they marched, through the woodlands, now. Many paid the price of discovering how well the Machist soldiers could see in the dark.

Then things started changing. After their once-an-hour five-minute rest period, some were culled out, apparently at random, and were taken off with a group of soldiers into the woods. This pattern, often with several groups going off in different directions, was repeated almost every kilometer.

Finally, well into the night, they stopped and were told they could sleep. There was mixed reaction to this development; it was welcome relief, but it implied another long march for most of them the next day.

Small trucks came along, as they had all day, dispensing little tins of water and packs of bluish-gray material, much like a half-loaf of bread in size and appearance, yet fairly hard and crunchy.

And tasteless.

But it was food, and they ate it ravenously, those who weren't too sick to eat.

Exhausted, most were asleep within minutes of eating.

If the exercise weren't enough, the last batch of water contained an additive to insure slumber, making it much easier for the hard-pressed soldiers who, nonetheless, seemed never to tire or need breaks themselves.

Soldiers awakened them after daylight. The man and the girl from the hotel awoke painfully, feeling every aching muscle. The residue of the sedative helped somewhat, but not much.

He groaned and stretched. She shook her head in an attempt to clear it, and looked around cautiously.

"How far do you think we've come?" she whispered to him.

"Not far," he replied in a low, cautious tone. "Maybe ten, fifteen kilometers at most, probably a lot less. You can still hear the screeches of gulls occasionally above the trees."

She looked up, trying to penetrate the forest and catch a glimpse of the white birds, as if seeing one would convince her that something real was left in the world. There were a few breaks in the foliage, but although she thought she heard them once or twice, they never showed themselves.

"How much longer are we going to walk?" she moaned in tired hopelessness.

He shook his head sadly. "I don't know. And I don't know what is waiting when we get there."

Suddenly he noticed one of the soldiers looking at him and shut up even though their captors seemed in a better mood, more relaxed than they'd been the day before. There were many whispered conversations and complaints in the group, but rarely did the soldiers move to stop it.

This was not, the man knew, a sign that the worst was over; it was, rather, a sign of extreme confidence in their captors. *Their* worst was over; they'd done their job efficiently with, to them, a minimum of trouble.

The small trucks came slowly by again, dispensing more of the blue-gray loaves and, this time, pure water. Many more were hungry now, and they ate the stuff with gusto. A few fights started when some in the huge population tried to steal food and water from their fellows, and these confrontations had to be broken up by the guards.

The man looked at the scene in disgust. How quickly we become animals, fighting each other for the enemy's enjoyment, he thought sadly.

About ten meters further back, Genji and Moira were also decrying their aches and pains. Moira looked like hell. There was no other way to put it. She had dressed for a different purpose, and now the flimsy pantsuit was showing wear and tear. Her hair hung limp and tangled.

She groaned and rubbed her aching calves.

"I don't think I can go on," she said softly. "They're going to shoot me, I think."

Genji was about to reply when he heard a cracking sound nearby, and they looked up to see a woman's figure suddenly outlined in a light blue glow, then dissolve into the air as a soldier holstered his weapon. The former press agent sighed. "It would be quick that way. My God! Who would have thought it would come to this?"

But when the guards came along, urging everyone up, to the response of moans, groans, complaints, and protests, Genji and the former model managed to stand with the rest.

The march began anew. As it progressed, more people had problems, and some were now being helped along by others. But more segments of the line of marchers seemed to break off and be led into the woods.

Soon they would run out of paths, out of places where the little trucks could service them.

By midday they were in the deep woods. From near the middle of the column, the people from the hotel were now almost the front. There was no indication as to where the others had gone, but they knew that their own time was coming. There were more soldiers ahead of them than civilians.

Then, suddenly, a dozen soldiers broke off and stood to either side of them. A few people filed past, then the man and the girl, then a few more, including Moira and Genji. Without warning, the soldiers broke the group of perhaps fifty off and ordered them into the woods.

They marched into the dark forest, crunching over leaves and stepping over fallen logs, which was tough going for those who had brought only sandals or cloth shoes.

After what seemed like hours, they broke into a pleasant meadow, panicking a few antelope. It was a small island in the forest, with rolling green hills and yellow flowers. In the distance they could see the mountains. A small stream burbled through the center of the meadow. They were marched to the stream, then told to stop and relax.

"End of the line!" announced one of the soldiers with a nasty grin, and they halted, some washing their faces in the stream's clear waters, others just sprawling out on the grass.

Six of the soldiers sat in a circle around the group, weapons ready, while the other six drank in the stream and generally surveyed the area.

"What the hell do we do now?" the man wondered aloud. None of the soldiers seemed bothered by the conversation, and this emboldened others.

"Looks like they're waiting for something, or someone," another man with a low, gravelly voice responded. "As for me, I don't give a damn anymore."

Others murmured agreement with that.

Moira sprawled on the grass and looked around. A pretty spot, she decided. And the march was obviously over for them. A good thing, too, she knew. This was about her limit. Had it not been for Genji, she might have given up before this.

But she wasn't going to quit as long as he still carried on.

Ironically, the same level of pride and ego had been what kept Genji alive and going. As long as she kept going, he damned well would, too.

The day suddenly grew dark due to something other than the lateness of the hour; the clouds were turning from their usual light gray to very dark, near-black. Thunder rolled across the meadow, and a wind came up and caused the trees in the distance to start a whisper-roar, while a thinner swishing sound arose around them from the movement of the grasses and yellow flowers. The temperature began dropping rapidly.

The soldiers jumped up and spread around them quickly, weapons at the ready. "You will stay there!" one of them ordered, and they waited for the rain.

A torrential downpour that was so intense it almost hurt came shortly after. The noise and the spectacular display of lightning so close around them terrified some, but any movement away from the tight group was met by a stolid soldier with his threatening pistol.

Then, just as suddenly as it had come upon them, the storm was over. The ground was a sea of mud, and they were all soaked to the skin and feeling the chill of the afterstorm breeze against water-soaked clothing and skin.

The soldier's uniforms hardly seemed touched; there was, it appeared, a seal that kept them dry. One of them broke open a pack and took out a couple of towels, and they took turns wiping their faces and hair. No towels were offered the group.

It was well past dark now, but the group still huddled wet and mud-caked from Ondine's humidity. Flashes and rumbles had threatened more rain, but what fell missed them, cause for only small thanks. The little stream had become a raging torrent, which some had used to clean at least a little of the muck off. Others just didn't bother.

Near darkness, the soldiers had broken out what looked to be a glowing rope. It was flexible, about thirty centimeters around, and easily a hundred meters long. Giving off a dull yellow glow that yielded a little light and no heat, it was looped around the spot where they rested and waited, with warnings that anyone who crossed the line would be shot.

Moira shook her head and tried to wake up from a bad dream. She peered around in the gloomy rope-glow at the misery in the faces of the others, and knew that she must look much the same. It humiliated her; all the worse because she had been reduced to *their* level, the common people's level, with no way to change things. Even Genji, the little nebbish. She'd told him to bring her some water and he'd told her to get it herself. She felt as if she were sinking, alone, helpless, friendless.

And she was scared to death.

The man thought the girl was asleep, and he leaned over and brushed some mud from her forehead and pushed back her hair. She smiled and opened her eyes.

"I'm sorry," he started, but she cut him off.

"Don't be silly. I hurt too much to sleep."

He chuckled. Strange, he thought, chuckling now. The human race seems to adapt to almost anything.

She had a sudden, quizzical look on her face. "You know—it's funny, but I don't even know your name."

He smiled. "Doesn't matter. For the record, it's Yuri. Yuri Alban. And you're Azure."

Her eyebrows went up. "You remembered! Now I feel doubly guilty." She paused for a minute, thinking. "Yuri. That's a nice name." She leaned over and kissed him lightly on the cheek. "I'm glad you were with me through this, Yuri."

"I'm glad, too," he whispered softly. He leaned back on the grass. *Funny,* he thought to himself, *how these things go. Here we are, torn from the lives and civilization that we know, sitting in the middle of the wilderness in the muck, guarded by creatures of unknown motives —yet this is the most human I've felt in fifteen years. I know I should be crying, like that hysterical man over there, or in shock, or despairing, but I'm not.* He looked around at the dim figures nearby.

The ones with something to lose.

A whirring, whining sound woke them up. The guards had let them sleep long and late. They were still sore, still tired, and still starving, but it had been a welcome respite.

The sound came from an enormous flyer, perhaps eighty meters around, wedge-shaped with a command bubble. The figures in the bubble were impossible to make out, but the flyer was Ondinian, a long-haul cargo craft.

They watched the vehicle as it stirred the grass some fifty meters away, hovering just a few meters above the ground. Hatches opened underneath, and three conveyor belts lowered and touched the ground. Almost immediately, large cartons began offloading. The flyer continued moving slightly forward, leaving the cargo in rows. In just a few minutes perhaps fifteen crates, several extremely large, had been deposited. Then, as suddenly as it appeared, the flyer was gone.

One of the soldiers came over to them, picking up the light-rope and handing it to another to take in.

"All right!" he yelled. "Everybody up! Lots of work to be done!"

"What about food?" somebody grumbled. "Any food in that cargo?"

The soldier showed no expression, but neither did he seem irritated or taken aback by the question or its tone. "Plenty of food for those who work," he replied. "First you break down the crates. Then we eat."

They moved off toward the supplies. The boxes were of unfamiliar design, but easy to disassemble without tools. You just pulled a set of handles in each corner and the outer cartons folded neatly back, revealing the close-packed contents: more of those blue loaves—a lot of them.

After the crates were unlatched the soldiers let them eat. Then the work really began.

The crates were prefabricated structures that needed only to be fitted and locked together, much like a puzzle. It took only two hours, with the soldiers' instructions, to assemble a squat little building that used an unfolded crate as its floor. A heavy-duty generator of some sort fit snugly inside, and there were lights, bunks, desks, some communications gear, and even what appeared to be a shower and chemical toilet. The guards, at least, were going to have things reasonably comfortable. Some large, heavy boxes marked with strange symbols were moved inside, but the prisoners didn't know what was in them.

A few of the people refused to work at first. The guards allowed this, but when food time came again they were pointedly excluded, and they were also herded off, away from the river, and denied water as well. The message was clear soon enough: no work, no food or water. Within only a few hours, there were no more holdouts.

A mild modesty crisis that seemed to amuse the soldiers arose that afternoon. Some people had taken advantage of the night to relieve themselves *au naturel*, but the situation was now different.

Pleas to use the chemical toilet were ignored, and the prisoners were told that such provisions hadn't been completed as yet. One woman used that as an excuse to start running for the trees.

Then they were forty-nine.

A second building was more complex than the first. A barren little place at first, its floor was later lined with cushions in regular rows, and there seemed to be a platform at the front, like a stage. They also moved a lot more heavy boxes inside, but the building's function remained a puzzle.

Next came a tentlike structure. Wooden poles unfolded and interlocked to provide side supports, over which a heavy cloth cap was stretched and locked, providing a roof but no floor or walls. A network of slender poles was evenly spaced at about two-meter intervals beneath the cap. They fitted into locking supports in the slightly arched fabric top, and were then driven into the soft ground. When the poles were in as far as a mark etched into their surfaces the press of a stud sent out anchor supports beneath the ground. They were solid as a rock, and could support a good deal of weight despite their thinness.

The next box provided them with a rude awakening. When it unfolded at the release of the last corner latch, someone said, "Oh, my God! Hammocks!" Yuri nodded numbly, looking back at the open structure.

"That open thing—that's for us," he said.

A detachment, meanwhile, had been working under a soldier's supervision digging a pit toilet and dumping lime in the bottom. It wasn't the pit toilet that upset the prisoners, but its location.

The guard's quarters were to the left, the other enclosed building was perhaps a hundred meters to the right, and equidistant from the two, forming a triangle was the hammock-barracks.

The pit toilet was in the center of the triangle.

One thing the soldiers did themselves. Five of them unpacked a net woven of the lighted rope material and strung it, fencelike, from guard's quarters to a post a few meters behind the open building, then to the other structure, and back to the guard's quarters. The hammock-building and the mysterious structure were completely inside the perimeter, while the guard's shack was outside but for the little corner with the generator, to either side of which the ends of the rope barrier were attached and interlocked. An additional rope barrier sealed off that corner and the generator from the diamond.

The rope fence was barely a meter high. It did not look intimidating, and the guards knew it.

One of them nodded to another across the way, and the generator hummed into life, lighting the fence. It was far brighter than the temporary barrier of the night before; even in total darkness, the infield would be lit with an eerie yellow glow. Additional lights were affixed atop all three structures in the diamond. The prisoners had surprised themselves, even though there were a lot of them and the materials were obviously designed to be assembled by novices.

The job appeared to be done before dark.

The prisoners were all called together for dinner and given more of the loaves they were now used to.

Then a hose was connected from the stream to the generator, and from there to a pipe which reached over the fence at a little over a meter's height. There was a small push-valve on it, and this was how you could release the water.

"You did a good job," one of the soldiers approved. They could never be certain if the same one was always talking and in charge or not, since they all looked and sounded exactly alike. "We are ahead of schedule. That is good. Now we must wait until they are ready to proceed. There are many, many, many camps like this. It takes time to get set up."

"What comes next?" a woman asked.

The guard smiled. "You will see. All in good time. Only one more thing to show you, and a few more things to do, and we can all get some sleep." With that he turned and approached the glowing, meter-high fence. "Watch!" he called, and they did as he jumped easily over it. Satisfied, he jumped back.

"Doesn't hurt us," he noted. Then he picked up one of the loaves and threw it just over the fence.

The loaf got almost directly over, then burst into flame in midair and vanished.

"The same happens to you if you try and jump it, or even touch it," he warned. "If you don't believe that, then you might try it. It would make a more effective demonstration."

They sat in silence for a while, considering it, as the guard again vaulted the fence. A couple of other guards were bringing out portable soft yellow lighting and setting it up just outside the perimeter, near the open building. They played with the fixtures in the gloom until they had eliminated just about all shadow.

The lighting was an unobtrusive soft glow, but it was clear that nothing would go on in the people's sleeping quarters that wasn't visible to humans and Machists alike.

The captives settled back outside to think.

"You believe that fence business?" one man asked skeptically.

A short silence followed, then Genji replied, "I don't think so. Sounds like a lot of scare stuff to me."

Yuri smiled. "Want to try it? We're *dying* to know," he said. Genji gave him a dirty look but said nothing.

Yuri found a rock and tossed it over the fence.

The rock expired violently.

"But why are *they* immune?" a woman wondered.

"Something they carry," Yuri speculated. "Something in their clothing, or boots, or maybe something they swallowed."

"Bullshit!" said the first man emphatically. "Let's see."

"*Junge! No!*" a woman screamed, but the man, a big, muscular fellow, ran at the fence and leaped. There was a brightness in the gloom, a reddish fire that swelled up, and then engulfed the man. He was gone.

Someone sobbed. Moira was suddenly overcome with the shakes; Genji just stared at the point of the fence where the man had leaped. Azure clung tightly to Yuri, who squeezed her firmly.

A guard came to their section and looked at the fence. He nodded, smiled, then leaped over and walked up to them.

"Good demonstration," he approved, and then drew his weapon. "All right, everybody stand up, line up in front of the sleep-hut, here."

Numbed, they all complied.

"Now you will all remove all of your clothes and put them in a big pile here," he ordered, making a mark with his foot.

There were several gasps and some protests. No one moved to comply.

The guard fingered a stud on his pistol, then glanced behind him. They followed his gaze. Two other guards stood just outside the perimeter fence with pistols aimed at them.

He pointed his pistol at a youngish, well-built woman close to him. "You first," he said.

Her face was set, grim, defiant. "No. I'd rather die," she responded proudly. He fired his pistol, but the

woman didn't flare and vanish. The weapon was on a
different setting. Instead she froze, her face contorted in
horrible pain. He released the stud, and she pitched
forward, breathing hard but still conscious. Others
moved to help her, but the guard motioned them back.

"Remove your clothes and place them on the mark,"
he repeated.

She looked up at him, hatred and fear in her eyes,
then got up, somewhat shakily, and started removing
her clothes. There were a few more object lessons,
but most didn't resist, either because they didn't want
their own demonstration, they didn't care, or they were
glad to get rid of their tattered clothing. Once done,
each was told to wash himself off at the water pipe.

Finally they lined up once again in the strange yellow
glow. The guard who had told them to disrobe changed
the setting on his pistol and sprayed the pile of clothing, shoes, and whatnot, disintegrating it. Then he
turned back to them.

"Now that we are rid of a defiant one, we should
tell you that the fence will no longer kill you. We have
cut the power. Fifty centimeters this side of the fence,
it will give a shock such as the pistol does. Only if you
manage to go *over* it will it get stronger. This is unlikely. Thank you. Good night," he added, and jumped
back over the fence.

"Animals!" Moira said suddenly, getting somewhat
hysterical. "They're making us into animals!"

"Maybe that's all we are to them," a man responded.

"But we've got to *do* something!" Moira wailed.

"What do you suggest?" another replied acidly.

"I think we ought to get into the hammocks and go
to sleep," Yuri told them quietly, and slowly they did
just that.

The mobile observers continued to broadcast. It was
surprising, really. There had been a number of fly-by
patrols over the bush, but no attempt to jam the bush
frequencies. The best guess was that Ondine was a
special case for which the Machists weren't fully pre-

pared; most planets didn't have this sort of radio network, or need it.

"You ought to see the view from the top of Mt. Labiana," came the voice over the little receiver. "Incredible. Every clearing within fifty kilometers of Lamarine is lit by that dim yellow glow, like ten thousand fireflies. The city itself is completely dark; you'd never know it was there except for some truck lights and lights in a couple of buildings they must be using as a command center. The big flyers keep going out to camp after camp, servicing them with something from a big warehouse near the spaceport." He paused. "Whoops! Long enough. Back later," he told the listeners he hoped were there, and shut down.

A short while later a woman's voice came in over a much weaker transmission. She reported what she'd seen in the camps.

Amara turned off the receiver to conserve power and looked at Sten Rolvag.

"What do you think it all means?" she asked him.

"I read a few books for a counterinsurgency course once," he told her. "Lots in there about how revolutionary groups and conquerors handled hostile captured populations. This fits the pattern. Appears either things are similar in other places or else they read the same books."

All five women clustered around him now, listening seriously.

"So what's it all mean?" Tani, the lawyer, prodded.

"Well, in the old days they called it brainwashing," he responded. "Sometimes it was attitude adjustment or something else like that. I know of a couple of cases far back in history where it was handled this way at the start."

"Just what do you mean by brainwashing?" Amara asked him. "Do you mean they will make slaves out of their prisoners?"

Rolvag chomped down on his ever-present but never-lit cigar.

"Well, I'd say no from what they've done so far.

See, what they do is take 'em down to the pits, as low as they can go. Then they offer 'em a way back to civilization—*their* civilization. If they change, accept the enemy's way, learn to think like him, act like him."

"But, surely they can't do that on such a massive scale!" protested Maga, the accountant. "I mean, *some* will fall into it, but—"

"My psych teachers said that the technique, if properly applied, was almost irresistible. And they've had a dozen or more human worlds to practice on, all with larger populations." He removed his cigar, looked at it, then stuck it back in the corner of his mouth.

"And as for scale—well, hell, there are fewer people on this whole planet than in most major cities on other worlds."

"It's horrible," Tani put in.

Rolvag sighed. "More than you know. If they manage to pull it off, we might wind up fighting our own people. And I don't know a damned thing we can do to stop it."

As he spoke, far above, a strange little golden egg-shaped object braked and approached the planet cautiously, then matched orbits with some floating debris about three hundred kilometers above the surface of the planet. The new arrival was too small for Machist defenses to notice.

Solfège

THE AUTOMATIC SEQUENCING BROUGHT HIM OUT OF the inactive mode into which he'd placed himself for the journey. He preferred to do that; otherwise the long, lonely trips led to intense brooding and depression. And that way was madness.

He began an all-band scan. The first few hundred signals he caught were all Machist, mostly automatics of one sort or another, and occasionally scrambled transmissions between the surface and the station ships in-system. A number of transmissions were point to point on the surface, but he could make no sense of them, as they were in code.

One thing was clear: all lifeforms registering below seemed to belong to the same general family. Whatever Machists they were using for occupation, they were very close to humans.

He launched a camera; it was too small to be picked up by anything on the ground, and he could store all its input for leisurely perusal in his egg. Resolution was quite good; he could pick out individual figures at a distance of more than twenty kilometers.

He saw what he expected to see. The manual they had fed him talked about the progression, the march, the camps, and here it all was.

It was clear from the number of Machist ships and

supplies down there that they had carefully calculated their needs. They had little in the way of men and matériel to spare for the project, and so were making everything count. He wished for just a dozen fighter-bombers. *That* would cripple them, perhaps longer than necessary. But fighter-bombers would never make it through the highly effective defense screen they had put up.

Yet, they *were* vulnerable. The right-sized force, with sufficient explosives and expertise, could hit them in the supply depots. And they'd done a nice job on the spaceports, all except the one at Lamarine—where they had blown a lot of structures that looked effective, but kept the landing pads totally intact. Hit their supply storehouses in the sixteen cities, disable that spaceport, and they were just as trapped as the rest of the population.

But whatever could be done had to be done from the ground. No chance of getting an air strike through that picket, although, when the time came, he could sneak in unmanned modules with the necessary weapons and explosives.

Yes, he thought, everything was right there. An easy project. If there were free people around in sufficient numbers to organize, train, equip, and hit those places in one simultaneous operation. But that would take time. Lots of time. Time he had to grant the Machists.

And time was the name of the game.

He wished fervently that he knew why the hell the bastards were doing what they were.

Ritornello

TIME PASSED IN THE CAMP, AND PEOPLE, BEING WHAT they are, adjusted.

There was some promiscuity at first, but the sight of nude bodies quickly paled as that situation became ordinary. Very quickly, they were given seeds and small plants, and allowed beyond the perimeter in the daytime to plant them. They were given no machine tools of any kind, only sticks and stones. Two who had been farmers at one point in their lives gave the others a few pointers.

There was some urgency to plant the seeds and do it right. They were informed that all the plants should mature within a few weeks to a couple of months. After that there would be no more loaves. They were expected to feed themselves.

Human feces was no longer consigned to the pit toilet, but was used as fertilizer to speed the growth of the plants in the already fertile soil.

One day a small flyer arrived in camp, and they were lined up for an inspection of some kind. A soldier who seemed just like all the others looked over each of them and gave them inoculations. They were told the shots would protect them against common dysentery and a host of other diseases.

The ship also brought the collars.

They were very thin and light, and could be form-fitted so one was hardly aware of them. They went around the neck and were sealed there. The collar was a receiver with the ability to store a massive charge from the generator. Remove it, and the discharge would kill.

The receivers were happy only when fully charged. Get too far from the generator, say a little more than a kilometer, and they would begin discharging, giving off increasingly nasty shocks. Turn back and the discharge weakened, keep going and the discharge would eventually be lethal.

Very effective, very efficient. After fitting the collars, there was no more need for the glowing fence—except for the lethally charged one around the generator.

Then came the ultimate insult. The guard building and the building of as yet unknown purpose were "wired" to be off-limits, and the guards left.

All of them.

There was not a Machist to be seen.

"Now why the hell would they do this?" mused one man.

"A demonstration of power," Yuri replied. "These little things," he noted, pointing to the thin collar around his neck, "make certain we can't go too far away. We've all tried doing so already, already felt the nasty shocks. Besides, I have the feeling they're short-handed and stretched thin. They need those people elsewhere."

"But what's the purpose of all this?" Genji wondered. "I mean, here we are, no clothing, grubbing for food in the dirt, livin' like monkeys or somethin'. Why?"

Yuri sighed. "I don't know. They provided only those things we couldn't provide for ourselves due to ignorance or lack of experience. Now we're living as our remote ancestors did. But why?" He was squatting, and he turned slightly and pointed to the mysterious third building. "And what's that thing for?"

The social structure of the camp developed rather

quickly. Yuri, because of his take-charge attitude and seemingly endless knowledge of a variety of subjects, became the *de facto* leader.

Many paired off. It hadn't escaped anybody's notice that there were twenty-four males and twenty-four females in the camp, but that wasn't the way the social structure evolved. Some women clung to other women, some men to other men, some paired off in man-woman fashion, and a few joined with nobody—or with everybody.

Yuri was hurt more than most. Azure's early dependence on him had vanished under the new conditions. Though she always treated him with a certain measure of respect, she was cool to him as she began to jump from group to group, trying to conquer every man and every woman sexually.

But never him.

No, they came to him with problems, to solve disputes, even to try to heal small wounds. They needed him, deferred to him, depended on him.

But they never thought of his inner turmoil, his human needs. It tore him apart inside. Yet he was powerless to heal the psychic wounds inflicted on him by camp life, by imposing *his* needs on the prisoners. He had too much respect for them as individuals and as human beings for that, far more than they had for themselves or each other or him.

Time passed. They tried to keep track of it at the beginning, but the effort proved a failure.

Occasionally a Machist flyer would come by and give them a look, but only rarely would it stop, and then only to check the generator, count the people, and, occasionally, tend to badly set broken arms and the like. Twice they gave everyone shots, which must have been effective, for despite the minor injuries, the cuts, and the unsanitary conditions there was little disease and no infection.

We're animals in their zoo, Yuri thought bitterly.

It amazed him that there were no suicides. Oh, two or three had tried that way out, but they'd been so clumsy at it that they'd been stopped easily. He knew they really wanted to be stopped. All you had to do to kill yourself was jump over the generator fence or rip off your collar.

The one person who attached himself to Yuri with what seemed like genuine affection was Genji. The little man was eager to help in every way. A bad lightning storm had set a small fire nearby one afternoon, and he'd done a good job keeping the campfire going since, even making an enclosure in the woods that was protected from the rain.

Moira had adjusted beautifully, charming a male and a female into a cozy little arrangement where they did most of the work under her direction.

Everyone's hair was growing long, and all the men had beards except Genji, who didn't seem to be able to manage one. Some of the women's hair was getting to be a problem; it was so long it got in the way.

Using stones and sticks, they managed to make some crude spears, which weren't totally effective. But every once in a while the group managed to spear one of the antelope that cautiously crept out on the meadow. It disturbed Yuri that many of the people, the products of civilization, took such delight in the animal's death, and joined in the stabbing until it thrashed no more.

The vegetables and fruit trees grew with astonishing speed. Yuri couldn't be sure, but he knew, even as a city man born and bred, that plants didn't grow that fast, nor bear fruit that quickly. They were rationed carefully, and their own seeds were planted in new ground.

The diet began showing on them, along with the effects of sun and work. Their skins became tough and bronzed, all traces of fat were disappearing, to be replaced by muscle. Even the excessively thin, like Genji, were filling out.

They were becoming savages—rather quickly, too. Fewer discussions about the past, the Machists, or the future were held. Talk centered on more practical things, the crops, making better spears. Huts made of leaves and sticks were becoming the place of preference to live in some privacy. Although even Yuri didn't realize it, they had become a tribe, and he, as decision-maker and ultimate problem-solver, was becoming the chief.

Naturally, this turn of events attracted Moira to him. He accepted her and her entourage simply because of his hunger for companionship and his pressing need for sex. And yet, he didn't like her, her imperious manner, or her unwillingness to do her share.

Even the sex was unsatisfactory; he could satisfy her, but she couldn't satisfy him. It disturbed her ego, but it bothered him more. That old feeling was back in spades: he could dominate human beings, he could control them, even empathize with them, but he couldn't join with them.

All over the planet the pattern repeated, with some variations. Some camps needed close supervision, some had massive suicides, some broke out into intratribal strife, and some simply collapsed.

But most worked, as the Machists knew they would.

The Machist command was a mixture of satisfaction and worry. This phase of the transition required a fairly long time, and they didn't have the time. Already Combine forces were probing their defenses, pressing a number of areas. The next phase should be a while off, but it couldn't wait. Time was pressing. Time . . .

Vibrato

STEN ROLVAG HAD DONE VERY WELL FOR HIMSELF. Slowly other refugees of the bush had come to him, and, in their desperation to find some sort of leadership, some rock of sanity in their new world, they had embraced him.

Not without some struggle, of course. Some had come and tried to take the mantle of leadership, but Rolvag was too swift, too cunning, to be overcome by such moves.

He was not above shooting a man in the back, either.

The Hurley Mama Caves had become the center of a miniempire ruled by the Viking Rolvag and his princess Amara, as tough and ruthless as he. The community, which included some children, was over two hundred strong.

Rolvag often wondered why the Machists hadn't found him or blocked the still broadcasting clandestine radio network. Certainly he worried a lot that so many people clustered in the caves area would attract attention from the occasional low-flying patrol.

But the Machists didn't come. Some close shaves, of course, but never anything serious. Some of his group managed a few brief patrols down the other side of the mountains to see the camps. The sight stunned and sickened them: people who'd once been a part of the most progressive civilization living and behaving like colonies of apes in a zoo, complete with pet collars.

"Ain't no silver collars on *you!*" Rolvag always reminded his people, and it never occurred to any of them, him included, that they were, in their own way, as trapped, primitive, and tribal as the captives.

Nor were they any trouble to the hard-pressed Machist forces, so limited in numbers and so rushed in their program. As long as they didn't cause problems, it was unlikely that Rolvag's band, and those of many others all over Ondine, would be disturbed.

They were irrelevant.

Rolvag suspected as much, but he was content, playing out his dream fantasy.

Until, one day, the stranger appeared. He looked human enough and wore no Machist collar. He was rather well dressed, really, in a hunting-type outfit. A strikingly handsome, dark-complected man with thick kinky hair who looked as if he had just stepped out of a renewal parlor in the old Ondine. He asked to see their leader and was ushered, at gunpoint, to Rolvag without much ado.

Rolvag, dressed outlandishly in skins, grass skirt, and loud sport shirt, chomping on his inevitable cigar —he had thousands hidden somewhere, it was rumored —stopped eating his mutton leg and looked up at the newcomer.

"You're the leader of this, ah, community?" the stranger inquired politely, as if he were a tourist just stopping by the mayor's office.

Rolvag eyed him suspiciously. Something smelled wrong; the fellow was a bit *too* clean and perfect to be here at this juncture. He was glad for his own sidearm and for the guns of his people, but nervous all the same.

"I'm Rolvag," he acknowledged. "Who're you, and where do you come from?"

The stranger sighed. "My name is Daniel, Mr. Rolvag, and I come from the Combine."

Rolvag threw the leg of mutton down like a hammer, shaking the table.

"Liar! The Combine scrammed months ago! A flea couldn't have gotten in after that!"

"I'm very good at getting into impossible places," Daniel replied matter-of-factly. "That's why they sent me."

A set of ideas hit Rolvag all at once. "You got any armament with you? Maybe a ship to get us out of here?"

Daniel shook his head. "No, I doubt if anything less than an all-out fleet attack could break through right now, but we're working on that. As for me, it's a one-way trip. I have a drone in orbit that can put me in contact with the Combine, but I—that is, we, since more of us are placed in different spots around the planet, all linked to the drone—came down in cargo capsules. They aren't meant for quick takeoffs."

Rolvag was almost relieved. "So you're stuck here with the rest of us. How long you been here?"

"Several months," the other replied.

Rolvag's sense of wrongness came back. "Impossible! You'd never look like that if you'd been out here only a few days. I think you're a Machist."

"If I were it'd mean you were finished," Daniel noted calmly. "I mean, if I'm here, and I'm a Machist, then they've found you and are preparing to take you out. Right?"

This puzzled Rolvag. He was used to acting, not considering the subtleties of things. The argument was unassailable, though; he just wished this fellow made more sense.

"So, if you're from the Combine, what the hell are they doing sending people in now?"

Daniel reached for his pocket and was amused to see all the guns come up. "Take it easy," he cautioned. "I'm only getting some paper."

Rolvag felt more unnerved by the other's manner. This was one very cool customer. It wasn't human to be that confident.

Daniel spread out a map of the front close up, then of the distance showing the telltale bulge, much as Admiral Hudkins had done for him. This much Rolvag could understand. The Machist position was held only by inordinate strength, most of it wasted. In the long run, Ondine couldn't be kept by the enemy unless it moved outward to consolidate its position and won, something which, considering the new forces massing on the Combine side as units became available, was unlikely.

Ondine would be liberated.

Curiously, Rolvag felt no thrill, no excitement at the prospect. When you're living in your dream world, it is never welcome to have it pointed out that you must sometime wake up to reality.

"When?" Rolvag asked seriously.

Daniel shrugged. "Not soon. Not for many months, maybe longer. Last estimate I got was a little over a year and a half from now."

"Uh huh, a year and a half," Rolvag repeated. "So? We can hold out that long, I think."

Daniel sighed. He understood the situation well— Rolvag was only the latest in a long series of petty dictators he'd had to deal with.

"Mr. Rolvag," he said in a concerned tone, "you must know what's happened to the rest of the people on this world. That's only the first stage. My information is that the second stage is getting underway now— the re-education phase. We're in a race with the Machists, Mr. Rolvag. A race for those people's minds. We can't beat them now, so we have to stall for time. Time's on our side. The more time we can give those people, the better it will be when liberation finally comes."

"Just what are you asking?" Sten Rolvag responded, feeling that he already knew the answer.

"The Machists didn't spare a whole hell of a lot of men and equipment for this project of theirs," Daniel told him. "There are sixteen supply centers, one

for each city, and only one serviceable spaceport—
Lamarine's."

"They blew that one up," the colony leader growled.

"They only made it look that way," Daniel replied.
"Look, we now have groups training, preparing to
blow thirteen of the sixteen supply centers. The other
two will be a matter of time, the free humans being
less numerous and poorly organized through there. But
I think we'll have them in line within a month. That
leaves Lamarine, and the toughest job, which falls
to you if you'll take it.

"I want to make this mob into a military force,
train it, arm it, and send it against Lamarine to blow
that supply dump and the four serviceable pads. Do
that, at the same time you blow the rest, and the
Machists are *our* prisoners until the Combine comes
to our liberation."

There was a strange gleam in Sten Rolvag's eye,
one that looked somewhat like madness.

"The rest of you! Clear out!" he snarled at the body-
guard. He turned, saw two of the women in the back
of the cave. "You, too!" he snapped. "This fella and
me, we got things to discuss!"

They moved out, and quickly.

Finally satisfied that they were alone, the self-styled
Viking prince relaxed, seemed friendly. "Sit down,"
he invited. "Have some mutton."

Daniel took the log bench, but declined the mutton.

"So you want to train my people to blow up Lamarine," Rolvag said warily.

"That's right," Daniel replied. "I don't see why—"

At that moment, Rolvag pulled his pistol from under
the table, and fired at the stranger.

The action caught Daniel completely by surprise.
He moved forward in reflex action, and the beam
caught him full, bathed him.

He'd been prepared for hunting rifles, but Sten
Rolvag had an illicit service revolver.

The Combine agent was frozen for a second, then

flared and winked out. Rolvag noted with irritation that it'd also taken out part of the bench.

"Damned Machist spy," he murmured, and he almost believed it.

Stringendo

The denial of technology phase is important as a psychological softener. Most people adjust to it, which is the first strong indication of the malleability of humanity. When social and psychological degradation becomes an accepted norm, barriers to much deeper alterations have already been partially lifted. The next step is a crucial one, one about which we know little because we can see only its effects. Our best guess is that, having lived the way they have, the captives are offered a way back to civilized existence, a way out of the dreary, filthy life they lead. To do so, they must fulfill a set of psychological goals. These goals are achieved by applied psychology and Pavlovian conditioning. Whatever the Machists do, it works in a majority of cases fairly quickly, and—as the group of primitives living in squalor diminishes—in almost every case in time.

—*A Primer on Machist Behavior*, p. 974.

THE FLYER ATTRACTED LITTLE NOTICE FROM THE group; flyers were always stopping to check on this or that. Even the fact that this one landed in the diamond wasn't unusual. The generator was regularly checked and serviced as a precautionary measure. By this point the tribal group was so conditioned to their territorial limits they would never have exceeded them in any case.

Two figures climbed out of the flyer, one familiar and the other much less so. They quickly grabbed bags like large suitcases from the hatch, then ran clear while the flyer sped away.

This *was* unusual, and noticed by some of the people working in the fields. One was dispatched to fetch Yuri.

Yuri was in the woods with a small group testing a couple of makeshift stone axes—sharp, flat stones tied to sticks with antelope hide that had been soaked, tied, and allowed to dry. They worked, although slowly and with a great deal of muscle power, for chopping trees.

A woman ran up to him excitedly. "Yuri! Yuri!" she yelled, then halted, getting her breath.

"What's the matter?" he responded, concerned. "Somebody hurt?"

She shook her head and gasped for breath.

"Some men—some Machists—have landed in the diamond! To stay, it looks like!"

He frowned. "How many?" he prodded.

"Two, we think," came the reply. "They unloaded some cases and went into the funny building. And that's not all! Only one of them looked like the old soldiers! The other looked different, dressed different!"

Yuri stopped the chopping. "Let's go see what's up," he suggested, and they all followed him like obedient sheep.

The sun was still up, but already he could see differences in the diamond. Lights burned in the old guard shack—and in the other building as well.

Many of the tribe were there, but keeping their distance, waiting for him. Genji cleared his way, and those with him joined the rest of the group. He continued to walk across the diamond, past the now covered pit toilet, and up to a position between the two buildings. The protective fence around both was still up, he noted.

There was no reaction to his presence at the start, which didn't surprise him but did serve to unnerve him slightly.

The door to the strange building opened suddenly, and a puzzling figure stood there. He looked like an older man, with thin, carefully clipped white hair and a broad, snow-white mustache. He had a ruddy complexion, and was dressed in a casual outdoorsman's outfit such as might have been sold in the old days on the boardwalk of Lamarine.

The old days, Yuri thought suddenly to himself. How quickly it becomes the old days.

The man's face was gentle and kindly, and his blue eyes sparkled. "Well! Hello!" the stranger called out to Yuri, in a rich, friendly, grandfatherly voice. "Come on over! You must be the leader of the group!"

He approached cautiously, one eye on that glowing fence.

Suddenly the old man snapped his fingers. "Of course! Of course! The fence! Hold on a moment!" He went back inside and suddenly the area of the fence in front of the door went off. Then he was back.

"Come in! Come in!" the stranger invited. "We have much to talk about!"

Yuri approached the open door, and the old man stepped back to allow him to enter.

It was much the same as when they'd built it, although the air inside was cooler and not at all humid. The place had air conditioning! It had been so long since he'd experienced it that Yuri almost shivered in the chill.

There had been other changes, too, Yuri noticed. The barren stage area was raised still higher; there was a comfortable-looking chair to one side, as well as some mystifying electronic gear in two portable consoles.

And books and recordings. Lots of them. They lined one side of the building. The contents of those other boxes they'd stored unopened their first day here, Yuri guessed.

"Who are you?" Yuri asked the stranger.

The old man shrugged good-naturedly. "What are names, anyway? You might say a supervisor, a trainer, a teacher, or, more to the point, your ticket to a better life. For a while, anyway, let's use the name Ponder. It fits, as you shall see."

Yuri was puzzled. "You're human," he noted.

Ponder smiled. "That term, as you will discover, has little relevance, but if you want to apply it in the most basic biological sense, then, yes, Ponder's human. Why? Does that surprise you?"

"All of this surprises me," Yuri replied.

Ponder smiled. "Why not invite the others to come in? You'll find there's room here without much crowding. Then we can all get to the explaining stage."

They sat in silence, the cushions now uncomfortably soft for them; the air conditioning felt strange. Ponder sat in the chair next to the dais; the guard, who now put in an appearance, took up station at the door. He had a small wand or baton with him, but no weapon.

Ponder looked the captives over with satisfaction.

"Well, now, let's first get *really* comfortable," he suggested, and reached into a box, pulling out small packages. "These aren't really good for body and health, but occasionally they're a treat." He passed them down each row. The prisoners unwrapped them, finding chocolate and confection bars inside. Only Yuri noted that all were of Ondinian manufacture; the rest were as excited as schoolchildren. They ate them joyfully, sloppily, and were soon wearing chocolate and goo on their faces and occasionally on other parts of their bodies. Nobody seemed to care.

Next Ponder passed out bottles of what proved to be natural orange drink. After so long with nothing but spring water, the taste was incredible.

"Now that you've all been refreshed," Ponder began, his voice filling the building, "let us begin."

He got up, started pacing slowly in front of the stage, noting the eyes following him. "By now you've probably concluded that the mean old Machists had tossed you out into the wilderness and promptly forgotten about you. Be assured that it is not so! Something on this scale takes time to set up, and personnel to accomplish. Well, now the waiting's over. You are about to embark on a process which might startle, amaze, and alter your perceptions of yourself and your role in a civilized society. We hope so. The end result is up to you, not us. It may be very short, or very long, or indefinite. That's up to you and you only. Participation in this program is required, but it has no time limit. It will take as long as it will take."

He paused, noted that they were listening attentively, curiously, but with just the slightest apprehension. That was good. Normal.

"First, let's go into what this is all about—not just this camp, or this program, but the whole thing.

"A very long time ago," Ponder began, "a great race reached the stars. But, before it did, it developed on its own mother world a system and a society that was unbelievably wonderful. When it broke the bonds of its birth and went faring into the galaxy, it discovered other thinking, rational beings like itself, other races, other forms. This ancient race went to embrace them as brothers, but discovered to its horror that the other races feared them, treated them as enemies, regarded them as monsters. Their reactions were animalistic; a great shock to a race that had long ago abandoned any trace of animalism.

"Soon, this race found itself in a shooting war it neither started nor asked for. Technologically more advanced than its adversaries, it conquered them. But what to do now?" Ponder threw up his hands in despair. He was a good lecturer.

"The only thing possible," he answered himself, "was to teach the conquered people how to become a part of the wonderful new civilization of the first race, to teach them the joys of life and to rid them of the animalistic behavior the conquerors had dreamed of beating, but had been unable to beat on their own.

"Oh, there were doubts. Doubts that such a vast project could succeed. And it took a long time, and a lot of mistakes were made, but it worked! It worked!" His eyes shone with fire. "A true interstellar brotherhood of unrelated races was forged. And, as this new combined culture expanded still further, it began to discover its uniqueness in the universe, and its mission. Every time they met a new race, the reaction was the same. War. They came to expect it. And, after victory, they faced a new set of challenges, for each race was different, and had to be handled differently. But our system has worked! There are now over *fifty thousand* races to the Machist Association, some very human in appearance, some extremely, wildly different—outside. Inside, they are one."

"And now it's our turn," someone in the back said less than enthusiastically.

Ponder smiled. "Yes, now it's your turn. And, to rid you of those psychological illnesses you are only vaguely aware of in your dreams, emotions, and the writings of your poets and philosophers, we had to start at the beginning again. On some primeval planet your ancestors developed from the great apes of the forests. So to this state have you been returned."

"Humanity's come a long way from the ape stage," someone objected.

Ponder smiled. "Oh, *has* it now? Look how easily you returned to that state. Remove the artifacts, the machines, and the soft products of what you call civilization and you revert easily to a pack of wild apes. A serious look at one another in this room will show you just how weak and thin your veneer of civilization really was." They shifted uncomfortably and murmured a little. What the old man was saying came a little too close. They were becoming introspective and self-conscious about their past few months' living.

Ponder reached over and picked up a stack of newspapers. "These are a collection of newspapers from the week before Ondine fell. And these," he grabbed another stack, "are the same week's papers from so-called civilized Authrarium. Anybody here from Authrarium?"

They looked at each other, but no one spoke.

"Anyone ever *been* there?"

A few people nodded assent.

"Well, they'll tell you, those who have, that it's a pretty typical human world, supposedly the best humanity can do. Let's see . . ." He leafed through a newspaper.

"The city served by this paper has a population of twenty-three million, crowded but not above average these days. We look through and we find suicides at the rate of five or six percent a year. Suicides! That's over a million people in that city taking their own lives each year! A million!"

He rummaged through the papers some more.

"Well, let's see. They appear to average about two to three hundred murders a week judging from the sample, and there are loads of other crimes. We still have rapes there, it seems. And thefts by the score! The papers don't even mention them anymore unless they're big or fancy or flashy!" He turned back and faced them, leaning against the stage.

"Ondine's much better, of course. But not much. Suicides, for example, are much higher here—so much so that a *lot* of technology was devoted to preventing them."

He sighed. "So what do we have? A society with all the nice things technology has to offer, and people still acting like animals. Even in economics—the strongest, fastest, cleverest get the fat of the land, while the bulk of humanity exists on the dole, rotting in little stamped-out prefab apartments while a huge amount of government is devoted to keeping them fed and entertained with televisors, happy drugs, and the like. Unproductive, unhappy, directionless, and who cares? So they kill themselves, or they react against society by stealing, mindless violence, and whatnot. Hell! You have it better living like apes!"

"It wasn't all that bad," Moira objected.

Ponder grinned bitterly. "Spoken like a true member of the elitist class. But, we'll see as we go along. We'll see . . ." His voice changed as it trailed off. He seemed lost in thought for a minute. Then, suddenly, he looked up at them.

"We'll begin a closer examination tomorrow. Nothing will interfere with your lives here. Work at staying alive, then come here. Here we will address ourselves not to the externals, to the technological face of civilization, but to what's inside each of you."

He stopped for a moment, then looked and sounded slightly apologetic.

"I regret to say that the process is not an easy one. That's why a guard is here." He nodded at the soldier standing at the door. "The wand he has is a trigger. Each of you wears a silver necklace. That wand can trigger the necklace. The guard knows the system we will use, and what has to be done. Ponder can't stop the guard, or influence the guard's actions in any way. It is a tool that, regrettably, sometimes needs to be used, and the guard's orders are explicit on when and how to activate it. Please keep this in mind. That's all for now, until tomorrow. You will be called through the necklaces; it won't hurt you, just give you an irritating tingle. When you feel it, come here immediately. The energy field will begin to tighten moments later and it will become increasingly painful. As an early warning, a loud whistle atop this building will sound one minute before the field begins to narrow. If you come fast, you will escape any discomfort. That is all."

Most sat still for a few minutes, and Ponder let them. Then he announced once more, "That's it for tonight. Please leave now!"

Some people got up and left, grumbling as the hot, humid air hit them once again. A few continued to sit. Ponder pointed at one.

"Go!" he ordered, and at the same time the guard pointed his wand at the man. He cried out in sudden pain.

"Go!" Ponder ordered again, and he went, quickly. The rest cleared out.

Ponder was satisfied. It looked like a fine, malleable group, intelligence generally above normal, he thought, which was good. The smarter ones were easier, and they would condition quickly.

The group didn't return immediately to their huts of leaf and stick, although it was after dark. Instead, they sat around in small groups, talking about what they had seen and heard.

Around Yuri sat Moira, her two sycophants, and, surprisingly, Azure. She continued to act friendly toward Yuri, continued to treat him with respect and even some gratitude, but she rejected his advances and had not gone to bed with him since that night in the hotel. It hurt him, not so much that she wouldn't have sex with him as that she would have sex with almost everyone *but* him. She treated him like a wise older brother, or father.

Genji came up after tending the fire, and the group was complete.

"What do you think it all means?" Moira's man, Harber, asked pensively. "You believe all that stuff?"

Yuri shrugged. "Well, we *knew* the Machists were missionaries. They said as much at the first contact. And he sure made some telling points."

"Yeah, but how do we know that *their* way is any better than ours?" Azure put in. "Maybe it's worse." Most nodded.

Yuri smiled bitterly. "I don't think that's the point," he told them. "It really doesn't matter. Look at us, here. Hairy, naked, dirty savages. Hair stringy, matted, tangled. Bitten by so many bugs we don't even notice them anymore, like the little gnats buzzing around us now. And we go from here to our crude huts, and tomorrow we'll tend to our poorly planted crop, go hunting for more food in the forest, maybe bag an antelope. And this is *it*. No rejuve, no medicos. Until we get killed by some accident, or we don't get there quickly enough to scare off a hungry lion, or we get crippled and can't pull our share of the weight. It's only a matter of time, and that *they* have on their side. Now they're saying to us, 'Okay, live like this forever or join us and go our way.' It's the only out they're giving. That's where they got us by the short hairs."

"Speak for yourself," Moira responded haughtily. "I, for one, can't see any difference between their way and this. Personally, I'll keep this. The Combine won't let us down. They'll come back someday."

Then it was Genji's turn. "Hey! You know how many human worlds the Machists have taken? Well, I asked, and it's fourteen. Know how many we took back? None. Zip. Zero."

The thought made Azure unsteady. "You really don't think they'd just leave us here—like this?"

Yuri nodded. "Probably. Or, when they got all the converts they could and got tired of spending time and money on us, take us and put us in a zoo someplace. Maybe mess up our minds a little so we really *were* apes. A great object lesson and reminder for those who *do* convert."

The thought appalled them. It was only a tiny step from their present condition.

Finally, Moira said, "Well, maybe we'll play along with them if we have to, if it comes to that, I mean. But I don't think anybody can convert me into somebody I'm not."

"I don't know," Yuri sighed. "I really don't know anymore. It's their game played by their rules, and I'm pretty sure of one thing. They've done this all before."

All over the camp, in small groups, variations on that conversation were being repeated. The greatest enemy, their own inner fear, was loose among them.

That suited Ponder just fine.

Rauco

DANIEL WAS FURIOUS, NOT ONLY AT STEN ROLVAG BUT at himself as well. That was the *second* robot he'd lost on Ondine through carelessness, or by misplaying the situation.

He thought long and hard about the tactics he'd now have to use. He couldn't be himself this time, he knew. Not at the start, anyway. Not until he'd disposed of that nasty pistol of Rolvag's, and maybe Rolvag himself. He needed those people badly; the whole plot fell apart without Lamarine.

Already there had been some trouble, too. The Crede group had gotten impatient and attacked the supply depot on their own. Most had been killed, and a few caught, so now his presence was known to the Machists, at least in one spot. Surely they'd be on their guard, knowing that the Combine was at large on the planet and that they were indeed in a race over the available time. He was concerned that it would drive the enemy to employ more desperate measures on the captive population, but he had few ways of checking that out.

Or did he? he wondered suddenly. He wished he'd had the presence of mind when he arrived to put one of his selves in one of the camps. Before the silver collars, before a newcomer would be suspicious even to the people in the camps.

Now that he knew the measure of Rolvag, though, he knew what he had to do there. He could just rage in and give a show of strength, but Rolvag's pistol would quickly demonstrate the limitations of that tactic. No, doing what he wanted would take subterfuge.

And Rolvag seemed to have one big weakness.

It was something Daniel didn't want to do, something he wasn't sure he *could* do, but it was the quickest, easiest, and sneakiest way to accomplish what he was after. And a group the size of Rolvag's would not be ignored forever, not with known human agents about organizing the uncaptured rabble.

His other selves analyzed and surveyed and picked and chose until they had the right model for the new robot. The subject was examined down to the smallest detail; there would be no telltale manicured perfection here. The walk, the voice, the manner were also studied carefully, without telling the subject, who was, after all, on another continent and would never know of this project, of the imitation.

The computer had no trouble duplicating the subject, but pulling off this coup still would be difficult. He would have to devote most of his attention to this one robot for the duration of the project, at a time when the other groups needed a firm hand.

But without Lamarine the rest didn't matter. He only hoped his acting ability was up to the job.

Sten Rolvag was having a party. He liked parties, and if he liked them—well, then, so did everyone else. Most of the people thought him mad, but they all feared and respected him and so went along with his whims. For the occasion they'd set up a long table made of boards, on which were dishes of various kinds. People had blankets spread out under the trees in anticipation, but none would eat as yet.

The Princess Amara, as she insisted on being called,

arrived first. Rolvag's Concubines, as his all-woman
armed guard was called out of his and their earshot,
bowed slightly in deference to her, and she acknowledged
their homage regally. She was dressed in black—
knee-length service boots, the mini bathing suit she'd
kept, and, tied at the throat, a silken cape made from
somebody's fancy hotel sheet. A black leatherlike belt
with her marine service energy pistol in its holster circled
her hips. She was a handsome woman now, well built
and strongly muscled. Life in the caves had improved
her body, but she had cold, dark eyes and a personality
that hardened her current situation.

She reached the table and snapped her fingers. Immediately a woman with a shotgun rushed up and handed
her a cigar; another woman lighted it with a burning
ember.

Amara eyed the food as everyone else waited impatiently; they were hungry, but Rolvag's Concubines
controlled the food supply.

Then it was Rolvag's turn. Fat and broad, wearing
hunting boots and grass skirt as well as his own pistol,
he looked like an ancient Polynesian king rather than
the Viking he imagined himself to bc. Only the huge
tangle of whiskers recalled his Scandinavian models.

Everyone applauded in the obligatory manner as
he made his approach; they really *were* glad to see him.
Once he had his plate filled, they could fill theirs.

And finally, they did, and roast wild pig and mounds
of vegetables disappeared fast into glad stomachs. After-
ward there was dancing, even an improvised bong dance
with a kettle instead of the steel drum, which His Majesty joined but Her Majesty disdained. She was busy
surveying the crowd, picking out those she'd have later
on. As a marine she'd had the usual sex depressants,
but now that they'd worn off she was insatiable. Rolvag
didn't mind. Although Amara liked both sexes and he
was a confirmed heterosexual, the women he favored
and surrounded himself with were more than adequate.
The important thing was that Amara had been there

when he'd needed her; they were bound by something other than just nightly sex.

The merrymaking continued well into the darkness.

Suddenly there was a disturbance, and they all stopped and looked as two of the guards came into view, marching a woman before them at gunpoint.

She was large, larger than Amara, and about as muscular, but extremely well built and kind of exotic, almost Latin. Her skin had been toughened by exposure to the elements, and there were some pits and small scars, indicating she'd been through a lot. She was naked, and there was a narrow, white ring-shaped discoloration around her neck.

The dancers fell back, and Rolvag walked out to the fire to meet her. She stood there, looking a little bewildered.

"Who are you?" he demanded of her. "What do you want here?"

She stood straight, as tall as Rolvag, and noted sardonically that his gaze was not really on her face but on the twin protuberances below her neck. Sten Rolvag liked them big.

"I am Elvandrille Samone," she told him, her voice rich, deep, and musical, a singer's voice.

Rolvag's tone became gentle. "Where do you come from, child?" he asked sweetly.

"I was—well, I was in one of *their* camps," she replied hesitantly.

There was a general exclamation of surprise from the crowd, and some murmuring.

"How'd you escape?" he asked her, genuinely fascinated. "I thought that ring," he pointed at the mark on her neck, brown but not nearly the deep brown of the rest of her, "killed you if you took it off."

She nodded. "It does. Or, it's supposed to, anyway. But I'd had it with living like that. Like a filthy animal, a monkey in a zoo. My brother and I decided to end it. We took each other's collar in our hands, and we pulled." There was great sadness in her eyes, and she looked down. "It killed him, all right—but I was still there. No feeling, nothing." She stopped for a minute, composing herself.

"I don't know how long I stood there before I realized what had happened. I don't know why, either. Maybe my collar was bad. Maybe pulling each other's collar off caused my charge to go to him along with his. He was standing back to the generator, shielding me. Anyway, I was free. I ran, made the mountains in a couple of days with the help of food from a few camps, and met a spotter there. He told me about your colony, here, and I just made it."

Rolvag nodded sympathetically, then turned to Amara. She smiled and nodded.

"What say you?" he called to the people. "Do we accept this poor girl as one of us?"

"*Yeaah!*" the crowd roared back, genuinely touched by the girl's story and her escape.

"Come!" Rolvag invited her. "You shall sleep in our cave as our guest tonight, and we'll find a place for you." He leered at her while they walked into the mountain. "I'm sure we'll find a place for you in our community."

If she noticed the look she ignored it, and nodded appreciatively.

There were several women in the cave, and she did notice that a couple of them gave her looks similar to Rolvag's. Then the big leader told them to leave for an hour or so, and sat her down on a cushioned bench.

"Let me get you some wine," he offered, pouring from a large flagon. "We make it here. Not the best vintage, but probably the best on Ondine at the moment."

She smiled and took the glass, and wasn't the least bit surprised when he sat just to her right.

"I'm sure the wine will be wonderful," she gushed. "I haven't had any in so long I've almost forgotten what it tastes like."

He beamed. The high-potency stuff he'd given her would work wonders, and she'd never know she was becoming drunk.

A couple of toasts, a couple of glasses, and she was

acting silly and relaxed. He put his arm around her, she put hers around him, and they leaned into each other.

Suddenly her hand shot out, ripped his pistol from its holster with force, and pushed him away violently.

He was surprised, even a little shaken, but as she pointed the weapon at him he laughed.

"So!" he roared. "All a trick, eh? Well, it won't do you any good! Go ahead!" he invited, picking himself up off the floor. "Pull the trigger! See what it gets you."

She pressed the firing stud, and nothing happened.

He roared with laughter. "A few others have tried," he told her. "They learned the same lesson as you. The pistol is matched to me alone. It won't work for anyone else." Suddenly the expression on his face grew serious, his tone nasty.

"All right, you bitch, now I'm gonna take what I want and then throw you to the wolves." He moved toward her.

She looked at the gun in frustration, then took it and squeezed it tightly in her hand. The blue crystalline structure crumbled.

Rolvag stopped, looking bug-eyed at the impossible.

"You shouldn't have killed my brother Daniel, you pompous, self-centered son of a bitch," the girl said softly, then reached out, striking him a knockout blow.

Daniel looked down at the unconscious form. He didn't feel at all comfortable or natural, but he'd accomplished what he had to do.

Partly. There was still Amara and the other energy pistol.

He went to the cave mouth, and, taking care not to show himself, adjusted the frequency on the oral simulator. Voiceprints of Rolvag taken by the ship helped, but he could never be sure if an impersonation was effective until it was tested. If it was off, there'd be a hell of a fight.

"Guard!" he called in Rolvag's voice. "C'mere and take this bitch away!"

He was right; the guard was never far from the cave mouth. Two women with shotguns entered the cave.

He leaped at the first one with enough force to ram both his body and that of the first guard into the second.

He rolled, was up before either guard recovered. One started to scream, but he cut her off with a threatened blow and picked up both shotguns, pointing one at the two women.

"What the hell *is* this?" one guard demanded.

He barely remembered to readjust the voice back from Rolvag's to the woman's one he'd used.

"I'm the liberation army," he told them. "Want to change sides?"

They both grumbled, and rubbed various parts of their bruised anatomies.

"Where's Amara?" he demanded.

One guard smiled. "Wouldn't you like to know?"

Daniel sighed. As uncomfortable as he was impersonating a woman, what he was about to do made him even more so. He forced the two women up and back into the cave. They lost a little of their composure when they saw Rolvag's still form, but held firm.

He had no magical truth serums, no hypnotic powers to draw them out or make them do his bidding. And time was running out. He had no desire to lose a second drone body to an energy pistol.

He tied one up and gagged her with some clothing he found in the cave. The guards were confident enough in their ultimate rescue that they tried nothing funny.

He picked the second guard for interrogation because she obviously took special care in her appearance. Vanity was an exploitable weakness.

He tied her hands and feet with more cloth, then kneeled in front of her.

"Listen good, honey," he told her. "I'm in no mood for funny stuff." He reached over, picked up a jagged crystal from what had been Rolvag's energy pistol. Reaching over for a small piece of wood, he made her watch as he drew the jagged piece along it, causing a deep mark.

Now he grabbed her by her hair and held the crystal to her face, just below the left temple.

"Oh, God! You wouldn't!" the guard protested. "No! Don't!"

"Tell me all about Amara," he invited.

"I—I can't. She'd kill me," the guard sobbed.

He pressed on the crystal, making a small scratch that drew blood. She tried to shrink from it, couldn't.

"Amara," he invited.

"You bitch!" the guard spat. "All right, all right!"

Daniel moved his index finger to her temple, could feel her heart pounding. He opened up his biomedical sensors.

"Now, where is she and what's she doing?"

"In one of the tents," the guard lied. "The big blue one below."

"Not good enough," he responded, and scraped the crystal a little more. "I can tell a lie when I hear one."

The girl trembled at the touch of the crystal and gave in. "She's in the cave below," she sighed. "She has two teenagers, a boy and a girl, with her."

That was the truth. He relaxed his grip a little.

"How many guards?"

"Two," she responded, again the truth. "Always two outside."

Daniel nodded in satisfaction, opened the guard's mouth, and stuffed some cloth in it.

Time was important. Soon somebody would notice the absence of the two guards at the mouth of Rolvag's cave and give an alarm. He didn't fear the shotguns and rifles even though they could cause inconvenient damage, but the energy pistol would be ready to destroy him.

He was sure there was only the one; it was the symbol of supreme power.

Besides, those things were hard to come by.

He carefully slipped from the cave and into the darkness. To avoid attracting Machist patrols, the so-called guerrillas used no lights and shielded their fires.

He adjusted his optics to low-light levels and the scene came in ghostly but clear. Climbing slowly and carefully down the path, he centered himself over the cave below. He could see the two guards plainly. Low-

ering himself carefully over the side, he hung by his
arms over them, and spread his legs. No matter how he
tried, though, he couldn't get both with one jump. He
wished he had his old, standard, familiar body; the
overlarge breasts he'd counted on to capture Rolvag's
fancy were inconvenient for this kind of work.

Silently he abandoned his planned leap and pulled
himself back up on the walk, turned and took a crouching position overlooking the guards. He was amazed
that he'd done all this and not yet been discovered.

Suddenly his hand touched a rock.

He smiled. Basic pitching might do it. He searched
for a second rock, found it, and just barely managed
to hold both in one hand. Although ambidextrous, the
robot had a lot of limits, one of which was the physics
of ballistics. A rock, thrown with force and accuracy,
required a follow-through of the body. So he would
need three seconds between the first throw and the
second. These seconds were critical, and his balance
was slightly off because of the unfamiliar body design.
Three seconds was time enough to give an alarm.

Well, time pressed. There was no other choice. He
sighted the guard standing to the left of the cave
mouth and calculated the distance, trajectory, and
velocity.

What he really needed, he thought, was one of Ondine's frequent thunderstorms, but you can't have
everything. He waited for wind and target positions
to get just so, then finally the moment came and he
acted with lightning speed.

The first rock struck the woman's head with extreme
force, propelling her off the ledge and into the blackness.

The other guard heard the blow and the body fall,
but the lack of an outcry slowed her for a critical
second.

She turned, brought her shotgun around, and took
a half-step toward the cave mouth when Daniel's second
missile struck her in the mouth, snapped her head
back, and tossed her, too, over the ledge.

It sickened Daniel to have to kill two essentially innocent human beings, but his was the practical, military mind that accepted it. There wasn't time to let such sentiments get to him—not now, anyway.

He jumped down to the lower path, a distance that would have probably snapped a real human's ankles, and eyed the cave mouth. The sounds from inside were those of a woman at pleasure. There was no sign that any of the commotion outside had been heard.

He slowly readjusted his sight to normal and crept to the cave mouth, which was covered with rugs so that little light escaped. He peered cautiously inside, and the sight disturbed him. So this is the glorious humanity we fight to save, he thought sourly. The kids seemed very, very young to him.

Well, anarchy had inevitably resulted in a dictatorship of the strongest, and the strongest were always corrupted by power.

He looked for the pistol, didn't see it. That worried him, since it took little aim to do a nasty job with one of those. *She* definitely didn't have it on her, not right now, that was for sure.

But she was a marine. He knew that from his scouting, from her general manner, and from the way she'd worn the sidearm as well as from the very nature of the pistol and her boots. The weapon would certainly be close to her.

The cape and boots were beside her air mattress and he stared hard. He needed telescopic vision now, but they'd never gotten around to providing that because he had the flying probes.

Can't think of everything, he reflected philosophically.

He thought he could make out a belt folded neatly behind the boots. That was the place, he decided. Aim for the boots and get the whole thing.

He estimated distances and considered risks. It would be about six meters in a dash, while she'd have to get the two kids off her to roll over to the pistol. Odds were one of the kids would be thrown in the direction of the boots, which wouldn't bother him much but would force her to reach over a very live and protesting body.

His ears detected the sounds of someone coming up the walk. Now or never, he decided. And acted.

It took just a moment before Amara noticed the figure dashing by at almost impossible speed.

She immediately jumped up, sprawling the two kids as Daniel had figured. One, the girl, cried out and landed on the boots.

Daniel saw in a flash that he was wrong. Amara reached under the air mattress and he dived for her left hand, landing almost on top of her. Her hand came up with the pistol, but Daniel's hand was holding her wrist.

Amara's marine training activated. Her right hand came down with a chop to the back of Daniel's neck, and though it made him sag, the blow didn't collapse him the way it was supposed to.

He squeezed, heard her wrist snap, and saw the pistol fall as she cried out in pain. Quickly he rolled off her, almost crushing the panicky teenage girl, and grabbed the weapon, crushing it as he had the first.

Amara didn't see. She jumped on the intruder with a snarl of extreme ferocity, and Daniel rolled over.

"Stop it!" he growled at her. "Stop it or I'll have to *really* hurt you!"

But she kneed the strange woman in the groin and tried to free her arms from Daniel's grip to deliver a body blow.

Daniel'd had enough. He pulled and yanked.

Amara gave a horrible scream and then collapsed, bleeding.

In his fury and haste, Daniel had pulled both her arms off, and she had fainted from shock.

He turned quickly to the two terrified children.

"Look!" he told them. "Go over and sit down!" The tone had such force that the trembling pair obeyed instantly.

This was *her* chamber, he thought. He noticed a

trunk with a small thumb-lock on it. He broke it easily, rooted through the trunk, found the marine emergency medikit he'd wanted, and went back over to the now armless, unconscious woman.

He worked fast. If he didn't seal the wounds quickly she'd bleed to death, and there wasn't time to determine her type and rig a transfusion from the kit.

The medipads adhered like skin, although they were just barely large enough to cover the wounds. Fitted to her, they'd integrate themselves into her skin, match it, and start repairs.

Next he gave her a series of shots for infection, pain, and shock.

The adrenalin actually brought her to for a groggy second. She looked up at his female form, wonderingly, and shook her head.

"Who—who are you?" she managed.

"Naval Captain Daniel," he replied softly. "Go to sleep. You've been relieved."

And she was out again.

This is one mighty tough marine, he thought with admiration.

Pianto

MORE ORANGE DRINK, MORE CHOCOLATE. IT WAS BE-
coming a regular routine at the camp. Only a few
days after the program had begun, all Ponder had to
do was sound the whistle and everyone would run to
his classroom, falling over themselves to get there. The
comfort, the relaxed atmosphere, the rewards, and the
pain of the collar had combined for quick conditioning.
He was in a hurry, and his early success pleased him
enormously; this was the best, most malleable group
he'd encountered to date.

He had explained to them the Machist philosophy.
It was similar to many utopian concepts, but it was
different in that, as Ponder kept stressing, it worked.

Basically, he'd explained, every Machist considers
every other rational being a precious organism. Every
one has something he or she can contribute to society,
and every one must realize his own value and the fact
that his life is interlinked with the lives of those around
him. The engineer and the mower of grass are worlds
apart in what they do and the skills they need, yet each
is an important, living, breathing, thinking being. They
must do their jobs because that is what they are best
qualified to do; there are no ranks or social strata in
Machist society, only jobs.

Everyone receives exactly the same in an independent distribution network. It is unthinkable to a Machist not to perform his job to the best of his ability, because to do so would negatively affect the lives of others. The system works of its own accord.

"Selfishness must be banished from the human spirit," Ponder told them. "You become a Machist when you think more about serving others than you do serving yourself. When everyone thinks this way there is a mental and emotional bond. No one is ever lonely, no one is ever friendless, no one is ever unappreciated. No one covets another's position, for all are regarded as equally essential.

"No one is ever alone," he stressed.

Books—and tapes for those unable to read—were provided to pound the philosophy into their heads. They were told to memorize the materials, and they had long discussions about them. These discussions were fast and furious; you couldn't fool Ponder, as Moira and several others discovered. You couldn't think that fast. You were caught in your own contradictions.

And many in the group aided Ponder's plan. Those who progressed were rewarded with special food and drink and with other minor rewards that were first resented by the others, then coveted by them.

After two weeks, all desperately wanted the rewards, the kind looks and favors from Ponder, and even the slowest began to realize that the only way they could get them was to actually think the way Ponder wanted them to think.

Even Moira started to crack after other women were given haircuts and allowed the use of combs and such while she was denied them. If the contradiction between the stated goals of Machist equality and the system of reward and punishment occurred to any of them, it quickly disappeared in the face of practical reality.

Soon, study of Machist principles became the primary work at the camp and food was provided in ever larger and more appetizing varieties by Ponder and the guard. The Machist teacher instituted regular strenuous exercise to counteract the sedentary habits they were developing. Men and women ran eight kilometers a day on a marked course in the morning, did an hour's set of various exercises, ran another eight, and worked out with weights.

And then they arrived at the next stage.

They sat at absolute attention in the little schoolhouse. Ponder looked at them in satisfaction. Some of them, in pretending to please, had become his favorite pupils.

He smiled at them.

"What do we say when we get up with the sun?" he asked them.

"We must think the correct thoughts," they responded automatically.

He nodded. "First, last, and always, that is the key. However, this is but the surface, the outer veneer," he continued. "Now we must face the hardest target of all. Our inner selves." He looked up at the people with that smile, noting their tremendous muscle development. In another couple of weeks they'd be strong as oxen, and they were beginning to look somewhat different from other humans. It matched their mental progress.

Everything had happened as they'd been conditioned to expect it, this time, down to the orange juice and candies. They didn't know that this time the orange juice contained a chemical used in human psychotherapy. It broke down inhibitions while it also made them open to suggestion.

Ponder smiled again, noting their expressions that showed it had taken effect. The dosages were correct; they would be loose and malleable, but they would remember everything clearly. It would have been easy to convert them with such drugs, but chemical doings could be undone. He was after a deeper change.

"Yuri Alban," he called out. Yuri looked at him and echoed his smile.

"Stand up, Yuri," he suggested, and the man did.

"Get up here on the stage, stand on the raised platform, and face the people."

Yuri complied, wondering all the while why he was doing so.

"Yuri," Ponder began, "you are the leader of these people. You are their father, their brother, their protector. Now you must tell them about yourself, your *inner* self. Tell us your life, Yuri Alban."

The gentle prodding and flattery opened up a floodgate inside him. He *wanted* to tell them, *wanted* to get it all out.

"I was born on Acheron," he began. "My parents were Traditionalists. A standard religious marriage. I was the only child they were allowed, and they raised me with kindness, although they spoiled me rotten. They were also overprotective. I was a little adult, never a child. I associated mostly with adults instead of with people my own age. I was never much to look at, and I was painfully shy around girls, so I never had much experience there, either. It was a kind upbringing, but a lonely one. No dancing, no partying, no moonlight drives, nothing like that.

"So I retreated into books and films and televisor material. I lived there, not just when I used them, but the rest of the time, too. My fantasy life became more real than my real life, even as I continued to do well scholastically. I imagined myself a big writer or producer, doing things everyone would read or see, hoping that if I got to be rich and famous people would look up to me, admire me, love me."

He paused for breath and then continued.

"And I did it, too! A big-time writer. Got invited to all the right parties, met all the right people, even met and fell in love with a beautiful model."

He paused again, getting a faraway, dreamy look more from the memory than the drug.

"Fawn was my fantasy. She was beautiful, and she was with *me*. I could see the looks of envy as we went places, basked in her glow as she basked in my fame and fortune. Everybody envied me. They used to come to me with their problems. Some of them were pretty bad, too. I stopped several suicides, helped out some good people with money, went out of my way to take them through bad emotional times. I really *cared* about them, and I don't know how many I helped."

His face clouded. "Then one day we—Fawn and me—went down to the 'visor studio to check on a script I'd done, and she met Hel Quaeder. He was tall and handsome and athletic, the perfect leading-man type, and he charmed her right in front of me. She left me for him a week later. A lousy *week* after five years!"

He started crying, and it was a few moments before he could stop.

"I fell into complete despair. I continued the act, the routine." He went on, voice quavering, "But it was no good. I just couldn't stand the parties with all those people making it while I just stood there, feeling alone.

"So I went to my friends, the people I'd helped through *their* bad times. I was despondent, I needed help, advice, understanding, *something*, as they once had needed it from me. And what happened? Friend after friend was too busy, too cold, or downright nasty and sarcastic. Not one was willing to help me, even listen to me, sympathize with me! For the first time in my life I realized how truly *alone* I was."

He broke down again. Many in the group were quietly weeping with him.

"Well, I tried to adjust," he continued, wiping away tears he'd never before been able to shed. "I'd keep going, keep working, but it just didn't work out. Every time I tried for any kind of emotional human contact, twenty bastards would zero in on her and I'd be alone again. Finally, I just couldn't take it anymore."

He looked out at his audience, focused on one of them.

"I came to Ondine because it was a beautiful place, a lonely place, a place I could die," he said softly. "I came here to end it. The pain was too great. And then along came Azure, there." He nodded to her, and she looked away, a slightly stricken expression on her face.

"She flirted with *me,* not even knowing who I was. We went out on the town, we *shared* a good time, a set of experiences, the ocean, the birds, the sunset and the afterglow. It wasn't just the sex, really—either I was pretty bad from being so rusty or I'd lost the capacity to divorce my mind from my acts—but the fact that she *would* have sex with me, that was important. And even though she's drawn herself apart from me, I can still feel affection for her for giving me a little hope."

Ponder nodded, a serious expression on his face. Azure, he noted, had lowered her head, was holding it in her hands. She was crying.

"Loneliness," the old Machist sighed. "You were half-complete. You shared with others, but they would not share with you. They neither understood you nor wanted to understand you. They saw only the outer shell, the superficiality, not the strong human being inside. Strong, yes, but unable to live without understanding, compassion, sharing. If you hold fast to the man that you are, you will yet join in that sharing, I promise you. You may take your seat."

He turned back to the crowd as Yuri sat back down, head bowed.

"Azure Pontine, take the stage," Ponder commanded. She looked up, tears streaming down her face.

"Oh, no! I couldn't!" she protested.

"Yes you can," Ponder replied gently, and helped her to the podium.

"I was born," she began, "on Alshustis. It's a dirty little world, a waystop for deepspace freighters. My mother was a prostitute, a good one. She was supposed to be fixed never to have children, but someone or something slipped up and I came out. I don't know why I wasn't aborted; I guess she just wanted to find out what it was to have a kid.

"Anyway, I looked nothing like her. She was pretty —really pretty. She shared a house with three other prostitutes, one other female and two males, and they were all the family I had.

"They did the best they could with me, I guess, what with business and all. I always had toys, and they put in a 'visor for me, and I grew up there. It wasn't bad, really, but I was so fat and dumpy and acne-ridden that the other kids laughed at me and made fun of me and my mother's job and all. I hated them for it, and kept mostly to myself.

"I came out early. By eleven I'd started growin' these big boobs, and by thirteen I looked eighteen. I thought at first of taking up Mama's business, but I was so ugly and they—the good ones, the high-class ones—were so beautiful that it seemed ridiculous.

"So I went out and tried to find some kind of job. Nobody asked my age, and I sure as hell knew how to flirt and shake the right places, and I wound up as the janitor in a travel agency. Not much of a job, but I was payin' my own way, sort of, and I got to meet lots of different kinds of people and see the promos on all those wonderful, far-off places.

"Well, one day a Lin Corporation man came in to drop some new promos, and I flirted with him, and he was a skinny little man with a goatee and a twitchy face that reminded you of a bird. And we went out, and danced, and talked, and all that, and when it was finished he surprised me by asking what I wanted most. I told him I'd love to see Ondine, and the next day I'm scrubbing the floor at the agency when he comes in and tells me it's all set, I got a job with Lin. It wasn't glamorous—street cleaning, really, an outdoor version of what I was doin' there—but it was on Ondine of all those promos and posters.

"I took it.

"Well, I got here to Lamarine, and it was *so* beautiful and gaudy and wonderful that I didn't mind the job at all. I got to know the boardwalk people, and I·had a different person to conquer every night! It was the only thing I had to meet new people.

"One day, I knew, I'd find my lover, the one who

would give me some direction, some purpose, who'd change my life. It was only a matter of trying. And there were some close ones, some ones I really thought were right. That kept me going, kept me encouraged. Until this takeover happened, anyway."

"So you used your body to meet other people, to try and find this perfect union?"

She looked at Ponder, moderately surprised by the question.

"It's all I have," she replied quietly.

Ponder sighed. "We think not. We think your low estimate of your own true value and worth has reduced you, in your own mind, to the status of a mere object, a utensil—your body. You think so little of yourself that you turned yourself into a thing. Don't look so guilty! It is all too common, sadly, and all too understandable. Loneliness again," he pointed out to the group. "This time combined with guilt, self-degradation, and, in the bargain, selfishness as well, for never once did she consider the feelings of others, even though it was because she considered herself so low and valueless that it never occurred to her that others might also be in the same predicament yet see her differently, as Yuri did. And *this* is the proud product of human civilization? Loneliness, misery, dejection, rejection, despair?

"Some civilization," he concluded bitterly. "You may sit down, Azure."

He called several others, each with their own sad stories to tell. One couple had been together for twenty-two years, yet found they didn't know each other, that they took each other so much for granted that they hurt each other continually, yet kept their pain to themselves.

Fifteen people had come up by the end of the session; fifteen people bared their souls to the rest. The scars were different, but they were substantial, and there were common points. The man who thought his whole life had ended when his wife and companion of many years, whom he dearly loved, was brutally murdered while walking home from work. The man whose group-marriage mothers treated him like dirt while lavishing attention on his sisters, and who had become an emotionally ravenous homosexual. The woman who'd never been able to relate emotionally to anyone, and, scared of sex, had herself neutered. Surprisingly, for so small a group, there was a man who'd done the same thing. And one sex change, from male to functional female, because she'd been a lonely failure as a man and envied the way women—to her eyes, anyway—seemed to have no trouble getting sex when they wanted it.

When they finally left that evening, Azure looked at Yuri for a moment but could say only, "Oh, God! I'm so sorry!" and run off into the night.

The members of the group spent the night mostly in silence, each thinking his own thoughts.

Exactly on Ponder's schedule.

It was a silent, sullen group that went through its exercises the next day, and for the first time many looked on Ponder's classroom with apprehension. Still, they obeyed the whistle.

They were too well conditioned to do otherwise.

The second session went much like the first.

Moira's kept man, Harber, proved to be a business-man who was fairly well pleased with his own success, enjoying the power and position he'd worked hard to get.

But Ponder pounced on him, asked him how he liked pushing around other people, how he regarded the people below him who actually did the work, and noted his contempt for the working class from which he'd come and to which many of the rest of the group belonged. The old Machist heaped mountains of guilt on the man, and, by doing so, exposed him to the rest of them. His justifications became more and more feeble as he looked into their hard faces, and he finally broke down and cried, actually begging their forgiveness.

This was better than Ponder expected; such people as Harber were usually the toughest to crack, although, once they did, they became the most eager converts of all.

The ninth name called in the third session was Moira Sabila. Many had been waiting for her name, and eyes followed her progress to the stage, noting her rock-steady demeanor. But she had changed radically. Her hair was cut very short, as everyone's now was, and it was turning from auburn to black. The once creamy complexion was now tough and leathery from the outdoors; the exercises were thickening her neck, waist, and legs as well as her arms, and her breasts seemed smaller, more a part of her overall muscular build. She looked more like a lady wrestler than a model.

But the imperious manner was still there, in her stance and in her voice. She clearly felt she had nothing to apologize for, or to fear.

"I was born on Venetoulis, in the Shaffer Cluster," she began, voice composed. "My father was a top fashion model who became a great fashion photographer after he became bored with the modeling life. He decided to have a child; not just any child, though. He had money, and influence.

"Sexually, he'd always been attracted to men. He'd often fantasized himself as a woman, even affected women's manners and clothing. So he paid for the extremely difficult job of cloning a female out of his cells—and for the extra genetic engineering to make that child as physically perfect as it was possible to be.

"Nothing was spared in making me his vision of the perfect woman. Since I came out of the tank physiologically adult, my childhood was mostly that of a standard clone's—special educational devices, special tutors and programs. I was walking in six months, talking in nine, and fluent in two languages by three. I never wanted for anything. Daddy doted on me, gave me everything. I was the center of his world.

"And when I went out into society, I discovered

I was the center of everybody's world. Heads turned and stared at me. Strangers, both men and women, smiled, and cast looks of dreamy awe and envy."

She paused, smiling at the memories and her own self-image, then continued. "I was different—and I loved it. The product of the best genetic engineering money could provide. I was the perfection others fantasized for themselves. Men worshipped me. Women reacted in much the same manner. I had no need of money, no worries of any kind. Legions always protected me without being asked; anything I wanted I had merely to mention and people would fight for the honor of getting it for me.

"Until this awful camp, my life was an endless series of beautiful places, beautiful clothes, beautiful people— although none so beautiful as I. I was designed for it, created for it, and I have loved it."

Ponder looked grim and slightly ill, although his eyes had pity. "And all of this innate superiority—people, all other people, are merely objects to you, aren't they?" he asked in a low, cautious tone.

"My superiority was designed, and proved by the way others reacted to me," she responded coolly.

"Well, maybe we should simply make beautiful sculptures, eh?" Ponder replied bitterly. "Lifelike replicas of perfection, so everyone could worship at their feet. And, you know what? They'd be better than you. They wouldn't *hurt* the people they came in contact with, and they would have just as much inside of them, in the human part, where it counts, as *you* do! NOTHING!" He screamed the last word.

"I don't hurt people," she fired back. "I bring glamour into their drab lives."

"Glamour!" Ponder almost spat the word out. "All you do is hurt people. You have never considered the feelings, the needs, of another human being in your whole life!" The charge didn't seem to faze her.

Ponder continued his attack. "And what's worse, in always regarding other people as objects, as things, as toys, you *never once* considered that that was all you were—a robot, a thing, a creature made in a factory for the express purpose of being everybody's plaything. You were not designed as a woman, *you were designed as a living sculpture by your artist father!*" That last hurt her. She looked at him strangely, but said nothing.

Now Ponder moved for the *coup de grâce,* while she was off-balance, defenses lowered as she considered the proper response. "You're like so many good-looking people," he told her. "You're all exterior. Nothing inside. No humanity. No warmth. No compassion. No regard for others. But—take away those beautiful looks and you're nothing. No, you're less than nothing, since everyone else is used to surviving as ordinary-looking people, while you—you have nothing!"

He reached behind him, and, with surprising strength, picked up a two-meter mirror and held it up to her on the stage.

"Look at yourself now!" he almost yelled at her. *"Look at yourself, Nothing!"*

At first she wouldn't look, stared down at the stage instead. But, slowly, under Ponder's taunts, as the rest of the group started egging her on, her head came up.

She saw herself.

Her mouth flew open, and stark terror came into her face. She raised her right hand to her face, feeling it. The image in the mirror did the same. Slowly the hand traced her new, squat, muscular form, while her mouth remained open, her eyes unable to break contact with the eyes of the image in the mirror.

"Nooooo!" she shrieked, almost howled, like a wounded animal caught in a leg trap. "Nooooo!" And then she rushed at the mirror, struck it, and continued to hit it, over and over again, screaming "No! No! No! No!" with every futile blow.

Ponder, who supported the mirror, seemed to have no problem keeping it up, showing surprising strength since Moira at this stage could probably bend an iron bar.

The mirror was made of plastine, a material that was

fairly light but structurally almost as strong as steel. Her blows dented it, pushed it in like so much tinfoil.

Finally, Moira collapsed. She just sank against the mirror, and down, onto the stage, head down, tears streaming. Then, slowly, ever so slowly, her head raised a little, and she looked out at the stunned audience with hollow eyes.

I'm like them, now, her mind told her. She fought against it, but the truth of the thought refused to go away, just like the image in the mirror.

Slowly, without even realizing it, she curled up into a tight little ball, and stuck her thumb in her mouth. Her expression reminded them all of a baby's, and she whimpered softly.

Ponder sighed and put the mirror down. He went over to her, touched her. At first she flinched, then she let him stroke her tenderly, as a father would stroke his daughter.

"Nice Moira, pretty Moira," he soothed, over and over.

She sniffled, then smiled. "Yeth, Da Da," she responded.

He looked at the rest of the people, feeling as well as seeing their pity for the stricken woman.

"We'll take a break," he told them. "Go on outside, leave her to Ponder. Go out and laugh and touch one another, hug one another, kiss and love one another, reach out to each other as this poor woman never reached out to anyone."

They filed out in silence, and, once out in the diamond, they *did* come together. They wept together for the poor soul of Moira, and they touched, and hugged, and knew in that moment that *they* loved, and cared, and would never be alone.

Back inside, Ponder sighed. He hated this part of the work. His work and mission was changing these people; changing them, he knew, for the better. He was committed to that.

But some people could only be destroyed.

He turned from Moira and opened his medical kit.

It was a large locker, one of those he'd brought with him. Several vials contained or had contained the drug for the orange drink, but there were vials for other drugs as well.

He took a vial and slipped it hesitantly into his injection-gun. Another drug from human psychotherapy, rarely used. He wouldn't have used it if there had been more time, but his orders were clear. In the case of Ondine, it was the only drug to use in these cases.

At least she'll be happy, he thought sadly. And she'll cause no more misery in others.

He leaned over, hesitated a second, then injected it into her rump. She jumped a little, but didn't otherwise protest.

He waited. A minute. Two. Five. Now he began to see some changes in her. She was more relaxed, smiling. She closed her eyes for a few seconds, then they opened briefly and stared blankly into space, before finally closing again. She sighed, and was limp.

Ponder gently picked her up and placed her in a depression at the back of the stage and covered all but her face with a blanket. Then he called the others back in.

They came in as one organism, smiling, eager, most of them holding hands. But, after they were all in, it occurred to them that Moira wasn't around.

"Where is she?" many said almost in unison.

Ponder's expression was grave. "Still here. Sleeping. She'll waken in a little while. No, don't worry, we won't disturb her." He sighed. "But, in one sense, she is truly gone. We ran some tests on her, and treated what we could, but she was just too fragile once her armor was stripped away. She cannot survive mentally without it."

"Do you mean," two or three people asked, "she's become that little child?"

Ponder nodded. "Probably forever. I've fixed a few things. She'll remember nothing of her past, nothing of what she once was. She'll speak as a child, act as a child would act. She'll be a child as long as she lives." He didn't mention that this was more a function of the drug than anything else. Had she gone catatonic, she'd have been an automaton, following any order without thought. As a regressive she'd still be open to suggestion.

He saw the sadness and pity on their faces.

"Don't be so sad," he told them, trying to sound cheerful. "After all, which among us would not love to be a child? She'll be a happy child, a good child, an obedient child, and she'll need constant love and care which you—which all of us—can provide. We can't all be perpetual children—else, how would the technology function, the comforts and care be provided? But she can, and will be." He looked up quickly.

"Will you accept her that way? Will you adopt her? Will you make her the loved and wanted child of all of you?"

And as he fired the questions they responded in unison, "Yes! Yes! Yes!" He felt better.

"Very well, then. There is no need for sadness, only for joy and love. Now, let us expose the last of our demons," he told them.

The few remaining were more of the same, with no real differences. The one thing they had all learned was how similar their emotional anguish was, if not in cause then in effect. It bound them together. A good group, Ponder thought, pleased. No suicides, excellent reaction, and only one mental breakdown.

And then, finally, it was Genji's turn. The last to speak, he was nervous, awkward. He'd changed a great deal, too. Filled out, become muscular, thick and tough, with little physical trace of the scrawny little man he'd been.

"I'm Genji," he told them needlessly. "Genji Di-Morda. I was born in a tenement in Romanch, on Traggatalia. I was never much to look at—hell, I couldn't beat my own shadow. But, boy! Could I talk! Bigmouth, loudmouth, that was me. I could argue anybody out of anything. It's the way I stayed alive.

"I talked myself into a reading and writing school. Well, sort of. One of the instructors took pity on me after I gave her the snow job and taught me after hours. I guess the combination of the mouth and the pitiful look got to her.

"Well, anyway, I look at the fancy dudes and how they live. I look at the beautiful men and women that everybody makes over, and I say, 'Hey! That's for me!' But what can I do? I can't become one of 'em. That's what my mom and two dads tell me. Ya gotta be a millionaire to get redesigned, and there weren't many places you could do that anymore. Hell, I was smart, but no genius.

"So then I see that the beautiful people, have some not-so-beautiful people workin' for 'em. The only way in was the back door, since I had no way of even knowin' how you got in those jobs. I mean the drivers and attendants and such. The big shots had real people waitin' on 'em, not machines. Class.

"So, anyway, I find these two dames that fix models' dresses. I play up to 'em, the whole sympathy bit. Well, the combination of my big mouth and the impulse of people to mother me pays off. They take me in to do their own housework. Not much, but I can read and write and am pretty good with figures, and pretty soon I've got a job writing copy for their agency. I got myself attached to one client after another, a year or so each. Some men, some women." He paused, sighing sadly. "Didn't make no difference for me that way.

"See, they were all beautiful. Fantastic. Doors opened for 'em. The best food. The best hotels. Travel. Parties. And right there with 'em was good old Genji, stayin' in the same hotels, eatin' the same food—important, you know? Because I was other little people's only way to the biggies.

"Then came Moira. I fell hard for her. Everybody did. She took me on, and played with me. Knew it was torture for me to see her make out with other people, even twerps as nobody as me. But never me. Even here, in the camp, it wasn't different. When I saw her change, her looks go, no longer so damned perfect anymore, I thought, maybe, maybe now she'll come to me."

He looked out at them, eyes showing his inner pain.

"But she never did. And," he concluded softly, "I guess she never will—now. I never knew. Never woulda believed. I couldn't imagine that *she* would ever crack, not like that."

"And what are your feelings about her now?" Ponder asked gently.

"I pity her. I really do." He turned and looked at Ponder. "It isn't fair. People should have insides to match their outsides."

Ponder nodded. "That's what all this is about. Life—life under the old culture—wasn't fair. But if we make the *inside* the same, and we make it something beautiful, then the rest doesn't matter, does it?"

They all nodded. It was the key to the group.

"And you," Ponder continued, pointing at Genji. "Look at what you accomplished! Up from nothing, from the dole! An education! A job you got by your wits and improved by being good at it. You have more to be proud of, more solid accomplishment, than any hundred of those people you admired, yet you continued to consider yourself inferior to them. Now that you've seen their shallow fragility, and you're still here, still standing tall, you should know your true worth!"

Genji smiled appreciatively and stepped down. The others nodded and murmured sentiments similar to Ponder's.

The old Machist sighed, and faced them.

"Well, it's over. In these interviews, and in our follow-up discussions, we've learned about each other, our pains, sorrows, joys, hopes. We know more about each other than any human group back in the Combine. We understand. We empathize with each other."

He went over to the electronic console.

"Now," he continued, "we must use that knowledge to take the last great step, the step all groups must take sooner or later. The melding of you into one, into a single organism. Each of you with different tasks, but of one mind. A mind so common to all that you will be able to enter civilization with others and know that they, too, are all of that oneness." He flipped on the console, illuminating myriad dials and switches, and a keyboard.

"We will help. We will continue to help. The final step, though, you must do yourselves." He fiddled with the dials, then continued.

"First, you must remake your vocabulary. The singular must be banished from your minds. The only singular is the oneness achieved by the melding of minds. Words such as 'I' and 'my' must go; you are becoming a part of something greater. 'I' is a lonely word, and 'my' is a selfish one. To help you, as a teaching aid, we have adjusted those necklaces to react to the singular. Say it, and you will receive a mild shock, similar to a static electricity shock. It will sting, but it will not really harm you. A teaching aid, no more."

He turned, walked over to them.

"In our next series of sessions, we will aid the meld. To join with one another, you must think of all people as one, you must translate the semantic 'we' into your actual self-image."

The technique proved to be rather simple, similar in some ways to group psychotherapy sessions held on Combine worlds. A strong hypnotic drug was administered, the first time without their knowledge. One at a time, they were approached and told they were somebody else in the group. Yuri, for example, was told he was Genji, and Yuri *did* act like Genji, talked like him, walked like him, thought he *was* Genji. And the rest of the group was also told that he was Genji, and they treated him as if he were; they saw him as the other man, they believed it. Each one in turn was switched; the impersonations weren't always precise, for they became their own image of the other, but it was convincing.

The twist that made it work was almost diabolical. Ponder *told* them they were all under a drug-induced hypnosis, that he'd only fooled them into thinking they were each other. Yuri, for example, who'd been convinced he was Genji, was suddenly told that, no, he'd been hypnotized, fooled, he was really Azure Pontine!

And he'd believe it, and started acting like her. Physical appearance didn't matter, of course, because if he *believed* he was the woman, and everyone else was told to see him as the woman, then external reality had little to do with anything. The program was remarkably effective and every few hours they would become someone else.

After four days of this, no one, male or female, was certain who he or she was. And, as each of them became others, lived a little like the others, he carried over characteristics from previous impersonations.

The words "we," "us," and "our" which their collars forced on them became more and more natural, not only because the only way to keep from being shocked was to reorganize their minds to use the correct pronouns normally and naturally, but also because they continually experienced being one another. The role reversals caused a great deal of confusion and disorientation at first, but they were played out against the established routines, the exercises, the songs Ponder taught them, the dances they created to perform themselves. Together, there was always work to do, cleaning up the camp, dismantling the old, primitive base, and using tools dropped by flyers to erect comfortable sleeping quarters, a kitchen, and storage facilities. New implements and supplies turned their patchwork farm into a more professional one. And, from the time they awakened until they all went to sleep, they were constantly together, constantly busy, with no chance to get away, to think.

They couldn't be sure who they were, and they couldn't be sure who anybody else was; all they were certain of was that they were not who they thought they were and that nobody else was who they thought they were, either. But, within just a few more days, they had all—each in his own way and at his own speed—crossed a barrier: Suddenly it didn't matter to them who was who and who they were. When Ponder decreased the dosages until they no longer had any hypnotic influences, it didn't matter. They didn't know it, wouldn't have trusted the information anyway. Self-identity was impossible to determine, and they learned to live without it.

Ponder was well pleased. He hadn't even had to adjust the necklaces to eliminate names; names were irrelevant to this group now. Slowly, carefully, he adjusted vocabularies, limited and shaped their thoughts using disorientation and conditioning.

Despite the shortcuts, despite the time pressures, his group was almost totally Machist now. Almost. The rest still needed time.

Time . . .

Diatonic

THE CAVE DWELLERS OF THE HURLEY MAMA WERE stunned when they awoke. Daniel had worked through the night, knocking a number of guards cold and killing three more in the process, but he'd been successful.

Before sunup, all the food as well as most of the spare weapons and ammunition and over three hundred medikits had been moved into the caves, and he'd carefully placed materials from a secret cache near the settlement. Now he waited patiently.

The guards' bodies were discovered just after dawn, and this raised a general alarm which brought out most of the population, including the bulk of Rolvag's Concubines.

They found Daniel, still in the guise of the strange Latin woman, sitting relaxed on the ledge in front of Amara's cave, idly juggling some small objects.

One of the Concubines yelled for him to come down, and raised her rifle threateningly.

"Before you shoot," he called back, "I have all the supplies in these two caves, and I've lined the caves with these." He held up two objects, small yellow ovals. Almost idly, he tossed one—a championship throw—over their heads and into the trees beyond.

It exploded, and a tree toppled over.

He smiled sweetly at them.

"If you get me, the one I have set goes off. If you don't get me, I can toss this one in."

They didn't like that, and there were murmurs and a slight pullback of the crowd.

"Where is Rolvag and the Princess?" one of the guards demanded.

"The Princess was injured when I took her energy pistol," he told them, and there were shocked whispers. "Rolvag's tied up for now, and I destroyed *his* pistol."

They liked that even less. The guards, that is.

The people suddenly got a collective idea. "That means we're free of the bastards!" came the whispers, which turned into a roar. Suddenly the guards found themselves having to turn their shotguns on the mob rather than Daniel.

"Take it easy!" the mysterious woman on the ledge called to them. It took several tries to get them calmed down.

"You have me all wrong. You haven't been liberated. You've just changed bosses," Daniel told them.

The temper of the crowd changed again, and the guns were back on him once more. There were murmurs of "Machists" and "clear out" from the group.

"I'm no Machist," Daniel assured them. "I'm Captain Daniel, of the Combine Navy."

This revelation caused an even louder uproar. Daniel glumly reflected how stupid and malleable a mob was. This one had changed sides several times in three minutes.

"Then—then we're liberated by the Combine?" came a hopeful voice from the crowd.

"Sorry, no. That is, not yet," he responded. "They're coming, they really are. That's why they sent me here. But they need your help."

The prospect of liberation, of an end to their existence in the bush, and memories of wonderful Lamarine swept through them—the guards included. They wanted more.

"Listen, I'll tell you what this is all about," Daniel began, and proceeded to do so. He spared little, including the tale of how the *first* Combine agent had been brutally murdered by Sten Rolvag. Most of them had felt Rolvag was right at the time, but you couldn't find one willing to admit it.

He explained to them the need for time, the possibility of trapping the Machists without supplies or a means to get away, trapping them so they could be rounded up by the people themselves.

"Think of putting little silver collars on *them*," Daniel suggested, and they cheered. "The road won't be easy," he warned, "and we must do our part as quickly as possible."

He had them. They'd have marched on Lamarine in a minute.

"But you'd be massacred by those goon soldiers right now," he told them. "So we'll train. We'll have a basic-training camp right here. You'll be in the marines. And you'll be taught to use the funny little eggs here, and bigger stuff, and how to move it just so. And we want that to happen with the fewest possible injuries."

The little band had little loyalty to Rolvag, so was ready for a change. Many had misgivings, but this gave them hope, the promise of revenge, the promise of a future. They would go along with Daniel.

The guards were also ready to change sides, and the fact that Daniel looked like a woman actually helped. Finally a demonstration of what he could do in hand-to-hand combat and the bending of two shotgun barrels almost completely around made the conversion complete. They had little liking for or loyalty to Rolvag; they'd just liked to be the elite who ran things.

And they were, still.

He found several men and women who were former service people, and they helped the guards train the population. Mostly physical conditioning, which wasn't popular, some marksmanship, and lots of regimentation and discipline, reward and punishment.

Daniel's biggest surprise was Amara.

After his first big day, he'd returned to the cave

where she lay, recovering from her wounds. A few people had come in to clean up the place—and, incidentally, to attest to the presence of the strange-looking whirring explosives to the doubters below—and she was lying on the broad air mattress.

Daniel was busy checking the explosives and making sure that there would be room for the big stuff he'd ordered and which was due any day via fast module, first to him in orbit, then down to Ondine. He was aware, suddenly, that she was awake, watching him. He turned. "Hello!" he said cheerfully. "How are you feeling?"

She turned her head, looked at her armless right side, then her equally barren left. The medipack had worked in well; except for an ever-so-slight ridge of lighter color, she looked as if she'd been born without arms.

"Ashamed," she answered him.

He smiled, came over to her. Even armless, she was a beautiful woman. "I mean the arms," he said.

She smiled wanly. "Okay, I suppose. There are occasional twinges of pain, and the wounds itch a lot. I keep trying to scratch."

"Those are the nerves. Want me to deaden them for you?"

"No, no, that's all right," she responded. Her whole manner, her personality seemed different, almost as if she were a different person from yesterday's haughty tigress. "You know, I tried to get up and put out my right arm to steady myself. I could actually *feel it*. Of course, it wasn't there and I fell."

"That's normal," he told her. "When the Combine retakes Ondine, you'll be able to grow new arms."

She shook her head slowly from side to side. "I don't know. I think it's a punishment of some kind." She closed her eyes for a moment, then opened them again. "I can't believe what I was like. I come from a good home. Navy brat, really. Honor-class marine. And then I get here, and—" She turned her head away. "I must have gone crazy, completely mad. It seems like a nightmare now. I was horrible."

He sighed. "Don't condemn yourself too much. The repression drugs they give marines are pretty severe. That's why you're never given shore leave for more than seventy-eight hours—the drugs start wearing off at ninety. You go through decontam before a leave so they can let you down nicely. If you just come down straight, everything you've repressed inside you bursts out savagely. It's a shame, but those drugs are the only way to keep shipboard marines from going nuts."

She looked up at him. "If only I hadn't missed the ship! If only I had gotten the call!"

"Why didn't you?" he asked her.

"I—I was—you're going to laugh," she said.

"No I won't."

"I was riding every tram in the city," she managed. "Silly, isn't it? But in the early morning there's almost no one on them, and it's quiet and peaceful, and the fresh air blows constantly."

He nodded understandingly. After months confined to a ship, getting liberty in Lamarine while still on repressives left few outs. Gamble, swim, shop for souvenirs, little else. The repressives kept you from any sexual desires, prevented you from getting high, and, unless the proper go-codes were initiated, made you so gentle you couldn't swat a mosquito.

That left fresh air, and getting away from people and that crowded feeling you had too much of on the ship.

She was looking at him again, hard.

"You know, you're a strange woman," she said wonderingly. "I never saw anybody move so fast, or just ignore good body-blows. And your manner—I was watching you. Very mannish. Are you on male hormones? Or did you have a sex change?"

He laughed. "Sort of the last," he replied. "Actually, all this is a put-on. I—ah, one of my colleagues came in as a man, got zapped by Rolvag. We were monitoring the episode. We're all male, you see, but it was decided that only an attractive girl could sucker Rolvag. I was elected."

She whistled. "That's some lab you must have! If I had that face and body I'd be the top poster girl on a thousand planets. It's almost a crime to waste it like that."

"The process can be reversed," he told her. *"Will* be, sooner or later."

She shook her head glumly. "That's what I mean. Can't you just give it to me somehow?"

He laughed. "Not the way *we* do things," he replied lightly. "But don't worry. A pair of arms and you're plenty enough for anybody."

She smiled again and closed her eyes. He leaned over and kissed her.

Now why the hell did I do that? he wondered. *Damn! I'm not even really here!*

She opened those big brown eyes and looked into his.

"The moment we looked into each other's eyes there was a bond," she answered his thoughts. "You felt it. I felt it. I can't do much. Not even hug you. But . . ." She let her voice trail off.

And he *did* want her, want her badly. And he gave her what she wanted.

And couldn't feel a damned thing himself.

The training proceeded smoothly. There were the usual excuses, the impatience, the people who couldn't or wouldn't submit at all or couldn't get the hang of it, but this had been the problem of drill sergeants since armies immemorial, and what he *did* get was a well disciplined team of almost a hundred men and women who could be relied on to do a job. They *were* raw, and more would be killed in the operation than he dared admit to them for all his roughness, but he didn't have the time to train them right.

His probes continued to monitor the progress of the Machists. There had been roughly sixteen million people on Ondine when the enemy took it only ten months earlier; children, more easily changed, had been separated and lifted out in the early stages. There were not as many children on Ondine as on more diversified planets, but that got rid of over a million. As far as he could tell, almost another million who were aged or crippled or ill had been ruthlessly exterminated. Any rejuves had also been eliminated, another two million. About two million more had perished on the marches or in the early camps, from the conditions, the inability to adapt, guard cruelties, or suicide. And, about half a million had made it to the bush around the planet, or to the islands which the Machists never reached. Most were unorganized, eking out a hand-to-mouth existence under the most primitive conditions. Of this number, three in five had perished in the ten months from starvation, disease, or other causes.

The remaining nine million plus had been separated into camps, 187,346 to be exact, averaging fifty per. At an average two Machists per camp, that meant almost 375,000 of the enemy were at work on the planet, plus the few thousand at Lamarine spaceport and the supply depots, the flyer pilots, and the like.

The totals worried him, since the Machists had unloaded nowhere near that total during the night of the takeover even when all five spaceports were open, and nowhere near the number of transports needed to carry all those people and the enormous number of supplies (generators, prefabs, food, seed, and the like) had come and gone according to Combine monitors.

They had ten times the number of people on Ondine that they possibly could have.

And they were still nearly overextended!

He considered these problems over and over, and they made no sense at all.

Amara came into the cave. Although sex was a one-way street for him, even if he'd had the male body, he still was emotionally awash in her. He was actually thankful that the male Daniel wasn't around; it was more obviously nonfunctional in certain areas. He couldn't tell her what he really was, where his mind really was, that what she thought of as him wasn't a new biological development for espionage, but a machine.

That, he thought, was only part of it. He was alone, so alone, so cut off from humanity. And now here was someone he cared about, someone treating him like a person, relating to him as a person. It didn't matter, somehow, that the relationship was based on a masquerade on his part, based on a set of falsehoods, doomed to be exposed when reality intruded as it someday must.

He had learned a lot about himself on Ondine. He realized that he had no future, only an endless present. This tiny slice of the humanity and companionship for which he had hungered was enough, as long as it continued.

He looked at Amara. She'd refused clothing; she wanted the rest of them to see her armless body, to know she'd paid a dear price for the way she'd treated them. He doubted that she ever would have the arms grown back; her guilt was overriding, and being a cripple somehow helped her keep going. She allowed her food to be chopped up for her, but refused to be fed by others or to eat other than in public, where they could see their former mistress eating like a dog. Daniel disapproved of her decisions, but came to understand that these actions were essential to her in some way. And she'd become good with balance and with her feet; she could open lockers, pick up things, handle some of them.

She helped with the training and its planning. And the unwary villager who decided she was helpless or defenseless discovered her speed, her balance, and the powerful strength developed in those long legs. She needed that, too, the assurance of self-sufficiency, of purpose. And she needed Daniel, because he understood all those things, knew why she'd been as she had and why she had to be what she now was—and still loved her.

"You've been brooding again," she accused him, as

she took one of Rolvag's cigars from its case with her foot, leaned over, stuck it in her mouth, then leaned into a lantern to light it.

"You know I have a transmitter in my head," he responded. "I keep getting reports. Bad ones." He turned, looked into her eyes. "Honey," he said, "there are just too damned many Machists. And they are doing a hell of a job. Without such numbers they'd never have had the spectacular successes they've already achieved. Nobody, not Naval Intelligence, not the Combine, not me—nobody thought a people could be transformed so quickly. We thought we'd have a year minimum, maybe two! But they are already done in some camps, and more are being wrapped up every day! That means more and more Machists for Lamarine."

She nodded seriously. "I can't imagine *how* they do it, but I've heard the observer reports." She shook her head in wonder, remembering the gaudy strip of the Lamarine boardwalk, the high-rise apartment houses, the masses of houses. "They were normal people—no, they were more than normal. They were generally happy, or at least content, having a good time. Family people, and tourists. How do the Machists remake people's insides with so little, as easily as big computers and top cosmetic engineers remake the rich people's outsides? And so many!"

"We'll have to find that out when we retake the place," he answered pragmatically. "What's most pressing is that there are over 350,000 nonnative Machists on this world, and as they convert the people they are being shifted back to Lamarine. And every one is another potential roadblock to our own mission."

"They'll probably lift them out," she guessed. "If that spaceport's still in service when they finish, we'll never catch them. They get away scot-free."

He nodded. "And, if we don't hit quickly, there'll be too many of them in Lamarine to stop it." He sighed. "The weapons canisters are here. Not just the sample. All. They've been dropped to the fifteen other teams already, and I had ours landed during the storm two nights ago."

Her face was ashen. "You mean we have to go now. But they're not ready! Not yet! A few more weeks, at least!" she protested.

He smiled, understanding now Sten Rolvag's reaction to him the first time. How tempting to be in the position to say "yes" or "no," to let it go "a few more weeks, at least." How many? One? Two? Six? Sixty? How easy —and how tempting—to report failure, to tell the Navy that resistance groups couldn't be organized before the enemy became too strong for any hope of success. To go on, perhaps for years—up to two years, the last report said—until the big ships blasted a hole in the line.

Duty, a part of his mind chastised him. And he wondered, what duty? To humanity? Well, humanity had turned him into a machine, had robbed him of his own humanity. He was as alien a thing as those Machists, perhaps more. Nobody'd thought of *him,* except as an exceptionally sophisticated weapon and adult building set, a new toy for bright but idle minds.

He wasn't human. He couldn't love this woman the way a human would; his sexual desire for her came from memory and disconnected nerves, the way she occasionally felt her arms and hands. When he held her as he was doing now, hugged her as he was doing now, *he* wasn't really doing it at all. He felt her through sensors that gave more than enough information to interpret but far less than those in a human body. And when he kissed her, as he was doing now, those sensors relayed only the impression of her lips to a tiny transmitter, then up to a reflector, then to the tiny golden egg in which he was forever imprisoned in a crystalline case. A brain so augmented that parts of him were walking, talking, in fifteen other spots on the planet.

He was a machine; not just this body, but all of

him. A machine with human memories and ghosts of past experiences now denied him, a machine like the self-aware computers that helped govern planets. A machine who desperately wanted to be human, but was not, could never be. And this girl, crippled in body and soul as he was, although to a far lesser degree, was his only link with the human race.

He broke the kiss, and she breathed hard. "Whew!" was all she could manage.

He'd attack, and soon, because, although he could never be one of them, he *did* desperately desire to be human.

And that was reason enough.

"We distribute the weapons in the morning," he told her. "And start over the mountains in the afternoon. We hit Lamarine five days from tomorrow."

She sighed. "I knew that when you kissed me. And I'm going with you."

"Absolutely not!" he roared. "Hell, you'd be no good in battle! You can't use a rifle, can't fire a missile, can't even be support for a launcher!"

She smiled confidently, and responded in a soft tone, "I can carry a pack with the best of them, and march further with less wear. As for weapons, my speed and kicks are better in close fighting than any two of those village creeps who think they're marines. And I can fire a missile with my feet as well as many of these farmers with two arms. And you know it. And that's why I'm going."

She stopped for a moment, looking at him, but he said nothing.

"I know you could stop me," she acknowledged. "A dozen ways. But you won't—you know me too well. You understand me. You know I *have* to go."

And he knew she was right, knew he had no choice either way. He cursed the Machists, for pressing him. He cursed her, for acting the way she did, for knowing him so well despite all, for being herself—she'd go for the very reasons he loved her.

Too quickly, he thought, annoyed. Everything's moving too damned fast! Oh, God! If only I had some time!

Time . . .

Durchkomponieren

THE WOMAN WALKED SLOWLY IN FRONT OF THE SLEEP-place, eyes on the ground. Occasionally she'd find something small out of place, some patch messed up, another uneven or irregular, or some little bit of this or that dropped during the others' labors. She moved and worked quickly and methodically, knowing that another was behind her, trimming the grass precisely with a sharp blade on a stick.

She heard the others start singing over in the fields, and she and the mower joined in. She smiled content-edly—she always smiled, *they* always smiled, for there was much joy in them. They had rice now, and corn, and wheat, and even a few cows for milk and chickens for eggs, and soybeans for protein.

Occasionally, while she worked, a dark thought from the past would intrude. She remembered it, yes, but with pity. It was the unhappy time, the time of loneli-ness, the time without joy. The time when there was no sharing. It seemed so very long ago, and strange, as if it had happened to another person entirely. And it was. Who had she been? Who was this other person? She couldn't remember. So many of the labels flowed through her mind, and labels were bad things of the old way. That other person, whoever it was, had been alone, directionless, purposeless, seeking joy and never finding it, seeking love and never finding it.

Seeking *this,* she knew, and lifted her voice even louder in song.

The Child came skipping happily down the path, and the worker looked up, returning the smile. She remembered the Child, remembered *being* the Child, and the Child was her, and a part of her, and in her.

The Child stopped. "We will dance this dark in joy?" It was really more of a statement than a question.

"Yes," both she and the mower responded as one. "We will dance this dark in joy."

The Child's face spread into a wide grin, and she skipped on. She, too, had her function. She could wash down the cows, and arrange the straw, and she could fetch water and other needs for any worker.

They were almost finished now. There! The farm was perfect! She and the mower looked back at the cleaned and trimmed and smoothed diamond with satisfaction.

Almost like clockwork, the farmers were returning, their song growing louder and more joyous as they approached. And now, here they were, and she hugged the mower and the farmers and they all rejoiced in the Touching.

They all sang, "It is to cleanse the one that we go!" as they went to the showers.

Ponder—they no longer called him that, for they understood that he was as one with them, and that it was his function to teach the Way to others—smiled as he packed up and prepared to go. He and the guard were no longer needed here. They had done their jobs, performed their functions well.

Because of the time, there could be little sophistication in the development of Ondine. There was more potential out there than was being used, he knew, but it didn't matter. They were happy, together, one. His orders had been to take his group and transform it into a self-sufficient agrarian society, and this he had done. They had built the sleep-place themselves, from the native wood, and it was beautiful. So with the communal kitchen, made out of wood and hand-fashioned brick, with the metal for the grills and some of the implements, like the knives, the only thing supplied.

Supplied, too, were the animals, precious few but there was a bull for every ten villages and a rooster in every henhouse.

What he'd aimed for, what he'd achieved, was to strip them of their essential self-awareness. The concept of property, of ownership, was gone. So, too, the relationship of male and female. It wasn't ignored; they just didn't think of it. And yet, they *would* breed, he'd seen to that.

He'd gradually reduced their vocabulary, forcing them to use only monosyllabic words, and selecting even those. They were practical words, words that related to them and their group life. They thought little about the past—and it was darkly that they thought of it, so they worked to sponge it away—and nothing of the future. They existed, and they were happy.

They shared everything, knew each other's simple thoughts almost before they were spoken. Some contact had already been established with nearby villages whose people were absolutely identical to those here, although the experiences attaining that state might have differed some from place to place and person to person.

Pain would not deter them, for they would all experience it and all take it as natural. Even death—for they had no more awareness of themselves as individuals, but only as components of a group. There would be no sadness, for each one of them lived on in the others.

And each had a job, a function, or a set of functions. There was no insignia, no uniform, no leaders, either. It was like a machine, a simple machine, each part doing its job and knowing that it related to the welfare of the group as a whole. It was unthinkable not to perform the function, and each of them knew and could perform the function of any of the others in such a simple subsistence economy. And they *would* occasionally trade roles, if one were feeling a bit off, or, sometimes, merely because they felt so close that they often became one another without thinking about it.

Nor were they sad that Ponder was leaving, although they were going to celebrate his departure joyously. They knew his function was to bring the joy to others, and they remembered how many, many worlds full of the beings they had once been needed help.

The generator was shut down now, no more glowing fences and silver collars. They were self-programed now; they would not think the rebellious words because such words are not to be thought. They would not escape, because they considered themselves free, and escaping was an individualist thought.

They were children—singing, dancing, laughing children, but skilled and knowledgeable enough to provide themselves with all they needed and to build on it. But not machines. Not automatons, without emotion or feeling. They hugged and kissed and touched and laughed and rejoiced in it. Theirs was a life of pure, uninhibited emotionalism, over which a sense of duty and purpose had been laid.

The Child ran to him. They weren't very different from her, he knew, and they didn't regard her as being different. She did what she could do. And she was the most loved and happiest child of all times. But tonight the Child was a man.

Ponder hugged and kissed him, and he beamed.

"We will eat now," he was told proudly. "We will eat, and sing, and dance to the late-dark!"

Ponder nodded, and walked with him to the diamond. It was another example of transference. Someone else was being the Child tonight other than the Child herself. And, for a while, until another transference, this grown man would really think he *was* the female Child. And the fact that the Child would also be there, and perhaps another one or two, wouldn't bother any of them in the least.

Ponder smiled in true happiness and satisfaction as

he ate with a people who were the result of his hard work and instruction.

And then, they danced the dance of sunset, and went on into the dark, until, finally, the flyer came for him and the last of his equipment. They did not say goodbye; there was no need. He was in all of them.

It had been a celebration no different from any other. They always ended their days like this.

And when the fire burned down, they gathered and cleaned up like so many well-programed robots, each knowing his or her job exactly, and doing it precisely. The next day it would start again, but they didn't think of that.

And now, as one, they went into the sleep-place, all lined with straw, and they joined, emotionally, in the Feeling.

And at first light they would awaken as one, and go off to another beautiful day.

And, all across Ondine, the same thing was happening. Many thousands of camps had attained their state; most others were not far from it. There were variations: some villages fished, for example, but the system was not really different. Essentially, every village was as interchangeable as every person in it.

Had the Machists had more time, they would have established economic zones, and specialties, and an interdependent trading network which would have included factories and sophisticated technology. It was as easy to have factory groups, and building groups, and service groups, as it was to have farming groups if they had the time to sort out the skills of the various people, recombine them, and develop them properly— as they had on numberless other captured worlds, as they were doing, much more leisurely, on the other captive human worlds.

But they didn't have the time for more than this, and they had no regrets. They were confident that they had fulfilled their plan, that the processes set in motion were too far along now to be reversed.

The Combine hadn't guessed the Machists' final step, the one that would bring even more purpose to their mission. Time was on *their* side, now.

Time . . .

Dissonance

THEY HAD BEEN ON THE MOVE FOR ALMOST FOUR DAYS. Crossing the mountains had been the hardest part; the weaponry and equipment was heavy, and it was difficult to get the bulky stuff around even the wide bends on well-worn paths.

Daniel wished that he'd been able to drop the stuff closer to the target, but it couldn't be done. From the moment they'd reached the top of the mountains, they'd discovered how dense the population below was. Thousands upon thousands of campfires.

Amara had held up better than most of the rebel band, and she carried a heavy burden strapped around her. She was a definite asset to have along from a military viewpoint, Daniel had to admit. Some still remembered the old Amara, and kept going when they wanted to quit simply because she was a reminder of the alternative. Others—most, it seemed—regarded her with awe and admiration. If she, an armless cripple, could do it, could carry those loads, could keep on—well, then, they weren't going to be the ones to drop out. Not before *she* did, anyway.

And Daniel knew she'd never quit.

Yet, emotionally, her presence disturbed him. She was the most vulnerable of the group, the most likely to get hurt when the fighting started, and he resolved to keep her with him, under close watch and protection, at all times.

They relaxed, and she stood while he undid the straps around her chest and waist that held the launcher she carried, a device which weighed thirty-six kilos and looked something like a giant wood screw with a hole through its point. Amara weighed no more than fifty-five or sixty herself. She sighed in relief, and sank to the ground. He watched, and others watched while pretending not to, as she took a canteen in her feet, uncapped it with her toes, then brought it between the soles of her feet up to where her mouth could grasp the nozzle. Then, holding it with her teeth, she drank. Some of the water splashed on her, but the method worked. Finished, she lowered the canteen to her feet and actually rescrewed the cap.

"Hell, if she can't kick a Machist she'll bite him in two with those teeth and jaws," Daniel heard someone say, and he chuckled. It was true. When you have to use things for purposes you've never used them for before, they tend to grow stronger.

She breathed hard in relaxation for a few moments, then she turned and looked out at the coastal plain. They were most of the way down the other side of the mountain, and it was getting light.

She turned to him. "How will we get through *that* with all *this* without getting spotted?"

"If we can cover up in the next few minutes and avoid being spotted by the flyers, I can get us through tomorrow night, I think. Look out there," he gestured. Everyone nearby looked.

"See the lights down there? They're generator-powered. Not as many lights as there were when we first saw it, are there?"

They looked, and saw that this was so. The lights were widely scattered over the plain, while earlier they seemed to be more closely spaced.

"Know why?" he continued. "Because the early fires were natural fires. The powered ones—that's where Machists still live. I mean the enemy ones, that is. Those we avoid. They can report."

They murmured and nodded. There were several relatively large areas of darkness leading almost straight to the coast.

"But, Captain," someone said after a moment—he insisted they call him "Captain"; the alternative was "Ma'am" and he couldn't have stood that—"if no lights means the Machists have gone, then they must've done their work, right? I mean, my God! That was maybe seventy, seventy-five percent of all the lights we saw!"

They all knew what the man meant.

Daniel knew he had to rally them. "See those big lights over there?" He pointed to the still dark horizon. "That's the spaceport and Machist headquarters at Lamarine."

That cheered them a bit, but their feelings were mixed. Most of the people were *from* Lamarine, and the ghostly blackness where most of the city should have been reminded them of what had been lost.

It was Amara, with no ties to Lamarine or Ondine, who realized this.

"Remember, the Machists didn't get *us*," she said proudly. "What's done can be undone, if we're successful. Whether or not those city lights burn bright and happy again depends to a large measure on all of us."

They accepted this, and with that acceptance despondency turned to anger, to hatred of the enemy that had done this to their world.

"Now get this stuff under cover and get some sleep!" she told them. "We aren't going to be stopped this close to our goal!"

They snapped to it, and, when most had gone, she turned and looked at Daniel smugly. "See? What would you have done without me along?"

He grinned. "Okay, so rub it in." His expression turned suddenly serious. "But I'm worried. Worried for you. Worried for them," he gestured toward the raiders, "and terribly worried about *them*." He gestured at the plain.

"I wonder what they're like now," she mused, looking to the coast. "Can anything on this scale ever be reversed? I mean, completely?"

He shook his head sadly, and put his arm around her.

"No, not really," he told her honestly. "They've been through a hell of a lot. If the Machists had done nothing but herd them into camps to live like primitives for several months, the experience would have permanently changed them. No, we do it for the sake of those who didn't get changed—although they'll never be the same, either. And for the children, the future. There *can* be an Ondine again."

She nodded, and they were quiet for a minute.

"Daniel?" she said lazily, breaking the silence.

"Yes, hon?"

"What do you *really* look like?"

He chuckled and turned to face her. "If I told you I was old and fat and bald, would you believe it?"

She laughed pleasantly in that infectious, high voice of hers.

"I don't believe it," she told him, and they lapsed again into silence as dawn broke. Both were under a tree cover, and there seemed no need to move.

"Daniel?" she started again in that same soft tone.

"Uh huh?"

"You're a symb, aren't you?"

He froze, as if struck by lightning and his other selves all missed a step. His mind raced, trying to think of new lies, new ways to laugh it off, but he couldn't. He'd known this had to come, and better now than in the thick of battle.

"How long have you known?" he managed.

"Since the first night, I guess, although it took me a little time to put all the things together. Nobody built like you, bioengineering or not, could have that kind of strength and speed. And then I noticed you pretending to sleep. It's your worst impersonation. And I knew you couldn't feel the sex. I don't know how—it's *good*—but I just *knew*. And then I remembered that handsome stranger Sten shot. Too clean, too antiseptic. That's still close to what you really look like, isn't it?"

He sighed. "Yes, pretty much. The way I *used* to look, anyway."

Now it was her turn to be stunned. "You don't anymore?"

Of course she'd assumed that he was a real person, someplace. Symbs were illegal, but occasionally used by agencies like Naval Intelligence. Basically self-aware robots, they didn't have the linkages for complex actions, so for particularly dangerous things, such as bomb disposals, or impossible things where only a human would do, like some rescues in space, they'd take the person with the requisite knowledge and skill and imprint a duplicate on the symb. It was never permanent; it faded slowly unless renewed. And symbs always had a programed time-wipe in any case, for they *knew* they were symbs, copies, strong echoes of real people, and that was the worst of it.

Daniel's bodies *were* symbs, of course, but with a difference. Energy-linked to the incredible computer that was part of him, they were extensions, rather than copies, of him.

"I was a fighter pilot," he began, and he wound up telling her just about everything.

"What's it like?" she asked curiously. "I mean, being in an artificial body?"

"Not very much fun," he replied honestly. "Not like being in a real body."

"Are there many like you?" she prodded.

"No. Not that I know of, anyway. I'm the prototype. I *hope* I'm unique," he added.

She looked surprised. "Oh, I don't know. Being almost immortal, able to be all those different people at the same time, go anywhere you please, *be* anybody or anything you please, with all that superhuman power, having the knowledge and speed of a computer—" she sighed and lay back "—I think that would be fantastic. No human needs, no hang-ups, no sex hormones or trapped biology. You wouldn't need *anybody*."

He lay back, wondering how to respond, how to tell her, wondering if he *could* tell her in a way she would comprehend.

"You're wrong," he said at last. "Wrong about not having human needs, wrong about not needing anybody." He shifted, looked directly into her eyes. "Look, as a service brat and later a marine, you attended a lot of parties, right?" She nodded, and he continued, "Well, did you ever go to a party where you didn't know anybody, and you stood there, by yourself, unable to make friends with anybody, watching them all enjoy themselves while you just sat there?"

"A couple of times," she admitted. "When I was young, and used to go to all those dreadful affairs with my parents."

"Well," he went on, "suppose *every* party you went to was like that? I mean every time, without exception?"

"That'd be horrible," she replied, imagining it. "I'd stop going to parties after a while. Become a hermit or something."

He nodded. "Well, suppose you *had* to go to parties? Constantly. Day in and day out. And they were all like that."

She sighed. "I think I'd kill myself," she answered truthfully.

He smiled the grim smile of satisfaction. "That's what it's like. I'm at the party now. I'm at a party every bit of the time—maybe lots of parties at once. I can exist in the party, even act the life of the party, even wind up *running* the party—but I can never join it as a participant. Like with us. I *do* love you, Amara, if you can believe a machine can love. I want to be able to love you, to feel you as others can, body and soul. I want it so badly it's tearing me apart. I *need* you. But it can never be. I don't *have* a body to give, or receive, or even to touch you. Just a remote control system on a plastine copy of a person."

"There's more to it than that," she responded. "I knew you were a symb from the start. It didn't make any difference. We touched minds, Daniel. I never believed it was possible. Oh, I'd heard about it, and been told about it by others, but never me. Oh, I suppose I had some romantic notion that if your symb would fall for me then the real you, somewhere out there, would, too. But, now that I know, it *doesn't matter,* Daniel. Can you understand that?"

He couldn't. It mattered to him.

She sighed again. "I'll bet if they knew the problem they could do something about it. I wonder if they could put a second brain in that egg case of yours? Wouldn't that be wild? Kind of like sharing the same mind. Together. Forever."

"An interesting dream, even a beautiful one, a really romantic one," he responded. "But I don't think it'd work. Suppose we wanted a divorce? Suppose you didn't like it? Being cut off from humanity is terrible, but being able to see it, walk through it, and still not be able to be a part of it is sheer hell."

She shook her head. "It's something to think about, isn't it?" She looked at him hard, her tone turning serious. "Listen, remember this. I love you, Daniel. Nobody else. I'm a part of you, just as much as that thing I'm talking to. And you're a part of me. Nothing will ever change that." She chuckled suddenly. "It can't be lust, remember."

"You'll feel differently someday," he told her. "You have a future, and I have an endless series of presents. Don't cut yourself off from that future. I know *I'd* give anything to have one."

"This kind of present is good enough for me," she replied, and kissed him on his plastine nose.

They started across the plains at dusk, breaking up into small groups for easier movement, less likelihood of detection, and to insure that, even if things went wrong, some would get through. They were warned to avoid contact with anyone on the plains at all costs, and were given their rendezvous positions within the city.

Daniel, Amara, and four others he trusted went first down the most direct path to the spaceport and supply terminal area. About an hour in, a flyer came straight at them, red and green running lights clearly visible, and it swept over them so fast at treetop level that they didn't have time to scatter.

Daniel and the others were certain that they'd been spotted, but the thing whirred on into the distance and was gone.

"Do you think they know we're here?" Amara asked nervously.

Daniel shrugged. "I don't know. You never know about those things. We'll just have to see if there's any unusually heavy flyer activity as we press on. They may just pass us off as parts of their own groups if they don't get too close a look."

There was no choice, and they continued to press on. Each group had someone who'd lived long in Lamarine and knew the coastal rain forest well.

They came very close to some of the camps, and looked at them in wonder.

The places were identically designed; they were all in large clearings or meadows, some obviously stripped by machine just for the purpose of the camps. All had water sources; if one of Ondine's countless streams didn't run through the camp, a catch basin had been made for the abundant rainfall.

That rainfall slowed their progress, too, as one of the great thunder and lightning displays soaked them, turned the ground to deep, slippery mud, and stopped them completely for half an hour.

Daniel's group was near one of the camps when the storm hit. They watched carefully, afraid that they would be spotted in the lightning flashes. They'd taken a mild risk crossing an open area as a quick way around a swollen stream, and the downpour caught them in the middle. They flattened in the mud and muck and looked at the large barracks area where the people of the camp were sleeping bunched together on straw. One side of the building was open to the outside but the slanted roof extended far outward. The rain washed off the roof, landed a good three meters from the barracks, and ran into a channel which led to the stream.

The wind swirled around, caused some of the rain to sweep into the barracks, and awakened the people. It would have been natural for them to sleep through the storm; the sound of falling water was so commonplace that they had learned to ignore it. The water itself they could not ignore, and they stirred. Some moved to lower a thickly woven straw mat across the open side, just inside the roof cornice. It would be suffocating for any length of time, but it would keep them dry for the duration of a short storm.

"God! Look at them!" Amara exclaimed through the thunder. "They all look like fugitives from a weight lifter's convention. Are those two lowering the mat male or female? They both have bigger breasts than I do!"

Daniel saw what she meant. Although he couldn't magnify, and was experiencing the same strobe effect as everyone else due to the frequent lightning, he had better resolution.

"The one on the left's a man, the one on the right is a woman," he told her.

"Could've fooled me," grumbled another man nearby.

And, as usually happens, as soon as they had the mat completely lowered, the torrential rains stopped, almost as if someone had just turned off a faucet.

Daniel helped Amara to her feet with her heavy load. "Let's make a run for it before they get that mat back up," he suggested.

They needed no more encouragement. The ground was slippery, and Amara's surefootedness deserted her. She fell on her side with an exclamation. Daniel was right behind her, and, urging the others to the safety of the trees, he quickly unstrapped the launcher from her back, tossing it like so many grams of paper just into the trees.

"Did you hurt yourself?" he asked her, concerned.

She shook her head. "I don't think so. Just bruised my leg."

He picked her up and glanced back at the barracks for a moment.

And froze.

Between lightning flashes, he could see the whole village of farmers was moving toward them. Amara looked up and saw them.

"Oh, Lord! What do we do now?" she muttered.

"Fake it," he told her. "That launcher is a little too obvious just over there. I don't think they saw it, but if they did we may have to knock out the group. If they didn't, I'm not going to give away the other people and the supplies by running to them." He sighed. "Well, you've been wondering what they're like. Now we're going to find out."

The villagers approached the pair without any apparent fear, evidently just curious. The sight was strange enough—a tall, exotic-looking woman holding a slightly smaller, armless woman. Both were caked with mud.

Daniel looked hard at the muscular builds of the people. He realized that chemical and hormonal agents must have been used to get them to that state so quickly, particularly to develop the markedly masculine musculature of the women. They looked as if they were made of rock, and the least of them appeared capable of uprooting small trees singlehandedly. Daniel wondered if even his robot body could hold its own against such as these.

"We greet," said a woman whose voice had the peculiar characteristics of both male and female; a by-product of the hormones, Daniel guessed. "Come to clean, to rest," she invited.

Daniel and Amara looked at the villagers strangely, both thinking: *They are more alien inside than outside. These are the same ordinary people found everywhere less than a year ago, and now they are different creatures. How is it possible?*

"The one is broke," a man noted, pointing to Amara. His voice sounded almost identical to the woman's.

"Let me do the talking," Daniel whispered in Amara's ear, then started walking deliberately away from the others and the telltale launcher, toward the barracks area.

"The one fills needs," he attempted, mimicking the single-syllable, present-tense speech.

They nodded as they followed him in. "The one is in, not out," they responded in unison, as if reciting a litany—which, of course, they were.

Don't jump the gun and rush us, Daniel prayed to the remaining four in the trees. He risked a quick glance back in the low-light mode, and saw that the launch tube had been pulled in. He nodded to himself that at least something was going right, and hoped that the others had enough restraint and confidence in him to hold off unless they were really needed.

The group showed him the communal shower, and he washed himself and Amara. He put her down and again gave her a warning look to keep silent.

"We share our goods and our needs are one," one of the group told him, and he realized that they really didn't see any difference between the two of them and themselves; none that mattered to them, anyway. He understood, too, that they were offering anything he needed.

"We need not," he responded carefully, afraid that even his syntax might give him away. They were friendly and harmless now because it hadn't occurred to them that he wasn't a part of their new world. He didn't know how long this hospitality would last if he slipped up and they realized what sort of visitors they actually had here.

"We must be on our way," he told them. "There is need for us in a new place."

They understood that, too, and wished them well. He and Amara started to walk off through the mud-soaked field toward the darkness and safety of the trees.

They felt the group's eyes on them, but they didn't look back, walking purposefully on, anxious that suddenly one of the group would say something that would louse everything up.

But they didn't. The two guerrillas reached the safety of the woods.

Amara suddenly breathed a tremendous sigh of relief and almost sank to the ground. He caught her, supported her for a second.

"I thought that was it," she managed at last.

He nodded. "That sort of thing we could do without," he agreed. "But now we know what's become of the people of Ondine, and what the Machists plan for everybody."

A bit further in they met the other four, who welcomed them in hushed but excited tones.

"We were going to plug them if they made any move toward you," one woman said. "Geez! You both got nerve!"

Amara smiled. "I couldn't breathe, even, around them! It's so strange! And—to think that they were like us only months ago!"

That was the thought in everybody's mind.

"The bastards," said a man. "I'll kill a hundred of them for that. One of them creatures coulda been one of my wives, or business partners."

"I know it's grim," Daniel said, "but it's not like they'd just exterminated them all. They seemed at peace, even happy. They're not suffering anymore, at least."

"I been to a psych-tank once," the angry man responded. "Most of them was happy, too. Don't matter if they kill your body or your mind. It's all the same. Now we know. They wiped out the people of Ondine and left their corpses running around."

Daniel sighed. To the unreconstructed citizens of Ondine, it was the proper response, but for him—well, he'd seen the happy expressions, the togetherness, the touching, the feeling for one another that was obvious in the village.

He was their direct opposite, he thought. The Machists had killed the intellect and left the feeling, and the Combine had killed the feeling while expanding his intellect.

And he didn't know who got the better deal.

Sforzando

·

IT WAS ALMOST DAWN WHEN THE LAST OF THE GROUPS reached the rendezvous, a deserted warehouse zone between them and the spaceport.

The spaceport itself loomed ahead of them, impressively massive despite the collapse of the terminal building and other large structures in the first morning's takeover of the place.

There were four pads; huge, golden disks ten kilometers around and a good kilometer apart. The edge of just one could be seen from their vantage point in the abandoned space-freight terminal. The hideout was infested with mice, the inevitable rats, and lots of bugs; many of the windows were gone. Anything of value had been stripped from it.

"I don't want to hit the port in daylight," Daniel told them. "It's too complex an operation. I want to use the day to observe the entries and exits, the number of Machists around the area, access points, and the like."

"What if a ship comes in?" someone asked nervously.

"So much the better, if it's not filled with troops. Then we get a ship, too. One that'll never act against the Combine again. I wouldn't worry about it anyway, though. The observers say there have been no ships

156

in for over three weeks. I think the enemy feels it already has everything it needs here."

Daniel walked to the center of the large warehouse floor, took a rifle from one of the cases, and used its stock to draw in the muck while the others stood around in a circle.

"Okay," he said, roughly drawing a straight line. "Here's the coast. About ten kilometers. Now, we're here," he made an X back from the line about fifty centimeters. "The pads are here, here, here, and here," he continued, marking each around the X, "and the supply dump is over here." He made an oval to show the position of the large prefab structure that the Machists had thrown up on the other side of the spaceport.

"Now, my team will blow the supply depot. It shouldn't be too hard to hit, but you'll have lots of soldiers around, and probably lots of trucks as well. They keep these things guarded. We'll get in so close we can't miss, and spray as many torpedoes into the thing as we can. Once we do, all hell will break loose, and that's good. That means that the Machists will come running to the support of their people under fire. That'll draw them away from the rest of you."

He turned, pointed at one woman. "Oggie, when the dump blows your group must already be within striking distance of Pad Four. It's the farthest away. As soon as we blow the dump, the guards will start running for the big bang. Don't hit 'em or worry about 'em unless you are seen. Get your stuff in and pour it on as soon as you can." He looked at a whiskered man with long, curly gray hair.

"Foggy, you get Pad Three. Same deal. Now, the only thing you have to watch is not to take the tempting hideout under or behind the big tanks to the right of the pad. They're explosive, and if just one of you were spotted a single energy shot into the tanks would wipe you out. Stay away from them, or, if you get spotted, lure the *enemy* near the tanks and use the trick on them. Okay?"

Foggy nodded.

He went through the other two—for the thousandth time in a month—in the same manner. Somehow the tactics all seemed new, but the target was only a few hundred meters down the road.

They didn't need as much artillery to destroy the pads as they did the supply depot. The things were built on shock supports like giant mushrooms; two torpedoes into the base and the structure would collapse. He warned them to watch for flying debris, and to be careful about the pad surfaces when they toppled.

"The only thing that worries me," Oggie said seriously, "is your team. Oh, you'll blow the depot all right, but how the hell will you get out of there? It'll be crawling with troops. And they'll be able to bring in more from town."

"We'll have to worry about sneaking through the troops," Daniel admitted. "No way around it. As for town, though, no real problem. They seem to be head-quartered in the old hotels, mostly up and down the beach, with their center in the old Grand Lamarine Hotel, and the big hospital behind it. It'll take them a good ten minutes, maybe more, to realize what's happening and get organized. Another ten to get here. If we aren't out in twenty minutes it's all over anyway."

The final run-through concerned the getaway. "Small groups, singles, twos, threes," he reiterated. "If you can get back into the coastal park they'll have to march up and down through all their pretty little camps to get at you. Sure as hell will make a lousy impression on their new converts, right?"

They smiled. Most of them knew, deep down, that their chances of making it back were slim, but this was the only way they had to strike at the people who'd ruined their world, altered their friends and relatives, wrecked their lives.

After a while, Amara came over to where he was resting with his back against a wall and sat next to him. The waiting was the hardest part of all.

"You beat it when the attack starts," he warned her. "I'll catch up to you."

"The hell I will!" she shot back. "I was in on this party from the beginning, and I'm going through with it. I'm not letting you out of my sight."

He sighed, exasperated. They'd been through this discussion time and again.

"But you can't *do* anything!" he repeated for the hundredth time.

"I can do more than you think," she responded as she had during the previous ninety-nine arguments. "And in the getaway it'll be hand-to-hand, or hand-to-foot," she added, and gave a kicking motion with her right leg.

"Besides," she continued, "you can't stop me, now. You can't spare a guard, and if you leave me here I'll most likely get shot or captured."

He threw up his hands and waited for dark.

The afterglow had faded in the south, and darkness shrouded what was left of Lamarine. The spaceport pads were lit, of course, and there were lights around the supply depot's loading area, but they cast shadows that were deeper than the night. Daniel's team crept slowly to within a couple hundred meters of the four-story depot, gleaming white in the strip lighting that kept the loading docks in perpetual day.

Each of the four members of Daniel's team had a fully loaded torpedo launcher, and they spread as far apart as they could in the shadows of the buildings and isolated palm trees along the road.

"Four in position," came a call over the tiny communicators stuck in their ears. "Three ready," came Foggy's voice. "One ready," said Deater. They waited anxiously.

The depot was not busy, but occasionally a flyer would dock on top or a truck would lumber up to the loading docks. The place was thick with soldiers; there seemed to be at least fifty of the black-clad, rat-faced men around, and they were all heavily armed.

"Two, what's the problem?" he called impatiently.

"We're hemmed in," came the reply. "Lots of soldiers here, like they were expecting an incoming. We can't get a clear shot unless we're in the open."

That was bad. The Machists had obviously cleared away some minor structures they'd counted on for cover.

"Well, sit tight," he told them. "We'll blow the depot, and that should draw them off, give you a shot at it."

He paused, feeling the tension not only within him but in the others as well. Amara stayed close to him and down, crouching like a cat.

"Depot team, are you set up?" he whispered into the little transceiver.

"Just say the word, Cap'n," came a gruff reply.

"On my count. Ten . . . nine . . . eight . . . seven . . . six . . . five . . . four . . . three . . . two . . . arm . . . FIRE!"

Four hands pressed four studs and rolled to one side. Four sleek programed torpedoes sped like blazing blue-white cigars for their targets. The results were almost immediate because of the short distance.

Stage Ones blew with enormous force, spreading severe concussion and a near-horizontal minifirestorm. It looked as though the building had erupted at four points. A flyer on the roof flipped up, over the side, and crashed into a truck below. Daniel could swear the roof had lifted five meters and crashed back down again.

Now Stage Twos went, triggered by the Stage Ones. Blue-white globes formed in four places in the burning structure, and the areas the spheres touched simply ceased to exist.

They waited for the building to collapse. Most of the soldiers had been blown in various directions and there were only a few figures running about, yelling instructions to each other.

But the building, on fire and terribly punctured, stood. Noting that, the torpedo teams rolled back, retrieved their launch tubes thrown back by the first blasts, and shoved their spare torpedoes home. One misfired, but three did not, and the sequence of the first attack was repeated, this time with devastating effects. The building collapsed like a house of cards.

Amara looked around warily at the now brightly illuminated road area.

"I don't like this!" she screamed over the explosions. "It's too easy!"

"It's gonna get tougher quick!" he yelled back, and pointed. A truckload of soldiers was bearing down on them from the direction of the city.

The four torpedomen grabbed energy pistols and began a running, firing retreat. Daniel and Amara, keeping low, headed back to the shadows of the buildings as well, his two pistols firing repeatedly.

The soldiers spread out professionally. One would occasionally catch a beam, flare, and flicker out, but with an uncanny silence. No yells, no screams, neither of pain nor of orders.

Daniel looked back, spraying the area to cover the others. His aim was deadly, and he picked the Machists off methodically until they learned his position. Then he had to move with superhuman speed back to the shadows.

He switched to low-light mode and looked around as the corner of a building flared and vanished, starting a small fire.

He didn't see anyone, including Amara, and suddenly he was worried.

As he pressed back, more soldiers streamed in behind him, making him even more wary.

Suddenly there was a tremendous explosion, and everyone, including the soldiers, turned toward the spaceport. A huge pad lifted briefly into the sky, appeared above the ruined buildings for an instant, then fell with a tremendous roar. And then another!

Two! he thought with some satisfaction. He'd stopped firing, and managed to elude the pursuing soldiers for a moment. Frantically he looked around for the others, saw not a trace of them. Several hundred meters to his right, soldiers were firing at something or someone, and he noted with surprise that they were using tight beams. That made the energy bolt a cutter; a slicer rather than a disintegrator. Now that they'd grouped, he realized, the Machists had decided to try and take as many people alive as possible.

Still, easier said than done on tight beam against a running target. He could see that their target, who, thank God!, had arms, had been cut completely in two and was certainly dead.

Where is she? It was all he could think about for a moment, and he had to calm himself down. There was still a mission.

"Pad teams! What the hell happened to the other two explosions?" he called.

He finally got a response, against the sounds of whining energy weapons and close explosions. "Captain!" It was Foggy. "Four and one were blown, and four went up with such a roar it landed on three, and three went up of its own accord! They had 'em mined to blow themselves, Captain!"

Sure they would! he thought, feeling stupid. Just in case the Combine scored a surprise breakthrough they had to be able to cut off a marine landing force.

"What about two?" he called back, still hiding in a ditch, still watching the soldiers spreading out everywhere but in his direction.

"They're all dead, Captain!" Foggy yelled back. "Only three of us left. Them soldiers didn't run for the big bang. We didn't fool 'em. No more torpedoes. There's bodies all over, Captain! And them soldiers, they ain't human. No yellin', no screams. Catch one partway and he keeps comin'!"

"Do you have any more torpedoes?" he asked.

"Yeah, two, and one launcher, but I can't get at Pad Two without getting mowed down. I think they're toyin' with us, or worried about the torpedoes. They got us pinned down but aren't movin' in for the kill. Yet."

"Depot team! Amara! Anybody! Is there anybody left?" he called.

"Mage, here," came a woman's breathless gasping. "I've made it clean. Heading out."

"Did you see anybody else?" he replied, almost pleading.

"All gone," came the response. "Maybe not Amara. I saw her get hit, and they were on her in a moment. I don't know."

He sank, seemed to wither. He just sat for a few precious seconds, unable to function. *I can't even cry,* he thought emptily. Then, suddenly, he was enraged, enraged at all of them. Slowly, carefully, he began moving along the ditch in the direction of the spaceport. There were soldiers all along the road, and he knew he'd have to shoot his way past them. It didn't seem to matter.

Elsewhere on Ondine, eleven of the fifteen attacks on the other supply depots had been successful, after a fashion. Most personnel killed, five more of his symbs gone as well, but it was a victory all the same.

He looked at the Machist soldiers patrolling the road, peering about.

They're all symbs, too, he knew now. Simpler, less sophisticated than he, but symbs all the same. That's why they didn't react normally to stimuli, like running toward the first blow-up. That's why they kept coming when maimed, didn't cry out when hit.

And, probably, that was why he was still around in this body. The simplest programing for a ground fight or guard function would be to sensitize them only to lifeforms. That way they never shot each other, could pick out the target from among their own number.

They'd reacted to his firing at them, of course, but the moment he'd stopped he'd ceased to exist for them.

"Foggy? You still there?" he called.

"Yeah, Captain," came the response. "But I think they're gettin' tired of playin' games. We seem to be up against something they don't want blasted, but they're comin' in slow but sure. I don't know how much longer we can hold 'em off."

"Keep trying," he urged them. "I'm coming to you as quickly as I can."

He sighed, and gambled. The pad explosions had collapsed and dislodged the terminal wrecked earlier, and large blocks were strewn all over. Pistols at the ready, he descended boldly into the dark, then crossed to the street where a particularly large, jagged section of terminal superstructure lay across the road.

He was right, he saw with satisfaction. As long as he walked normally, and didn't get too close to any of them, they ignored him.

A minute more and he was around the piece. He glanced down the street for a moment, and saw, way at the other end, someone on a stretcher being loaded into a small van carry registration number B-31.

Amara! They wouldn't bother for a symb. He looked in the direction of the pads; the one still intact stood out starkly among the rubble and continuing explosion flares from the others.

And he took note of the dead bodies of the team, sliced up like so much raw meat, blood all over. He looked back down the road. The van was moving off now, toward the city.

At that moment the hailing frequency opened on board his egg. There was an incoming message. "Daniel, this is a Priority Order Change from Admiral Hudkins," said a voice. "You are to abort, repeat, abort the spaceport destruction," it told him. It sounded so distant, so cold. "Try and keep the pads intact," it ordered, echoing hollowly through him. "N.I. analyzed your reports on the captured people and decided to move. We are at this moment in combat for Ondine. Hold on, Daniel! We're coming!"

He looked in the direction of the disappearing van, now lost in the dark. Amara. They had Amara.

And then he looked back at the pads. He could sense the energy bursts from Foggy's people, see dead bodies, twenty, thirty of them, lying about. Dark shapes, perhaps half a dozen of them, crept on narrow beams toward Foggy's position.

"Too late," he murmured, anger rising in him, clouding everything but the memory of the disappearing van and the sight of the dead bodies. "Too damned bloody late!" he snarled, and ran for the pad.

In space, the golden egg shifted in its orbit, moved slighty, and deployed silvery wings to the full, soaking up the light. He felt the energy as it was transferred, beamed to him on the ground, the full energy and resources of the ship and its great computer flowing into the single symb.

He reached the base of the beam on which the soldiers were creeping toward Foggy's position, and grabbed the support. The soldiers spotted him, but were thrown off balance as he grabbed a thick support strut and pulled, twisted it like so much cardboard, lifted it up, and flung it to one side. The beam collapsed, crushing two of the soldiers. Four others were damaged to one degree or another, and he picked them off easily, then whirled to pick off several latecomers.

Then he jumped on top of the rubble, crouched and sprang, landing almost at Foggy's position, over twenty meters distant. It was a totally nonhuman act beyond the power of even an ordinary symb. When he landed with tremendous force, the three rebels whirled and almost picked off their own leader.

Foggy stared at where the Combine agent had landed. The concrete was cracked and chipped, and strips of skin were dangling bloodlessly from the captain's feet and lower calves.

"Jesus!" someone exclaimed. "I always *thought* she wasn't human!"

"Never mind!" he snarled. "Get the hell out of here! Give me the torpedo launcher and scram! I'll take it from here!"

They didn't argue, but scrambled hastily over the rubble, shooting at dark figures as they ran.

Daniel looked around at the mass of bodies illuminated in the spaceport's eerie light.

"It's not your spaceport anymore," he told a Naval Command that did not hear it. "It's not your goddamned spaceport anymore!" He looked at the bloody dead. "It's *theirs*."

He judged the distance and angle of fire from where the bodies lay. Satisfied, computer checked and scanned, he ran onto the open tarmac.

The soldiers were slow to react; they were momentarily fooled by their basic programming. But, once they were able visually to see that the symb was not one of theirs and was carrying a torpedo launcher, they started firing.

The computer that was Daniel threaded a path through the crossfire at a speed almost too fast for the eye to follow, running right at Pad Two. On the run, Daniel raised the tube and pressed the firing stud.

The torpedo plunged into the base of the mushroom as Machist beams sliced him to pieces. When the pad blew, it took all of them with it.

Polyphony

UNLIKE THE DEAD AND DYING, DANIEL WENT ON. He registered and activated the polyform around one of his four unused symbs. He used his standard male shape for time's sake, but left it neuter. No sense in wasting time on realism. He was launching it toward Lamarine even as he was reporting on the raids, and on the total destruction of the pads.

The navy was understandably upset, but couldn't do anything about it except be philosophical. The fighting was rough; even though they had gambled in taking a major ship of the line from each defense zone, the Machists were putting up a hell of a fight. They wouldn't retreat; you had to knock them out completely.

He understood this even as the shuttle tube impacted in the water just off the beach at Lamarine, inflated, and popped up to the surface.

The Machists were symbs. They were *all* symbs. But they were basic ones, not remotes like him. Somehow they had to be periodically renewed.

Somewhere, he knew, was the source of the symb pattern. Somewhere, in Lamarine, there was probably no more than one, but certainly one, real live Machist.

He swam to shore quickly, considering the fact that he didn't know what a real live Machist looked like.

Or what it was, even. Would he know one when he saw it?

He was suddenly seized with self-doubt. Suppose a real Machist looked like the soldiers, just as his own symb looked like the original him? How could he know the real one?

No, he decided. The Machist would definitely be nonhuman. Those soldiers and the teacher dolls—the Ponders—were just models to make them seem more familiar to their prisoners.

But how did all those symbs get here? he still wondered. And how were they programed?

He didn't know, but he wanted to find out.

He felt certain that the Machist would be near Amara. For some reason they'd tried hard to take prisoners. The Machist leader wanted live ones if possible. Why?

If *he* got one, Amara or not, it would be the hospital they'd use. He walked up the beach determinedly.

There was nobody about. Symbs didn't swim, of course, or enjoy other luxuries of life. Probably, most of them were deactivated, wiped, stacked for shipment or destruction.

He crossed the boardwalk near the Hotel Grand Lamarine, all lit up and looking busy even from the outside.

I'll *bet* they're busy, he thought with some satisfaction. Destroying stuff they didn't want captured, mostly.

There were still mysteries here, although they were secondary to his personal concerns.

Who or what were the Machists? Why did they wage war over planets? How did they so thoroughly alienate a normal human population from its own people?

And why?

How the devil did they get three hundred and fifty thousand symbs on Ondine in a single night? How did they renew them, keep their patterns live?

And why Ondine? A planet they could never hope

to hold, and which held little of any value, human or
material, compared to more tempting targets.

He reached the hospital entrance. There were a
large number of vans and ambulances, including two
flyer ambulances, about, but no sign of their drivers.
He looked over the vans carefully, remembering the
big number he'd spied on the back of the one that
sped away.

And there it was. Van B-31, an Ondinian van
that had serviced the hospital before the arrival of the
Machists.

He looked in, saw two soldiers and a Ponder. The
two soldiers were obviously guards and well armed;
the Ponder was working some sort of computer console
in what used to be the reception area.

The windows said nothing; the rooms were all lit;
stretches of blank wall hinted at the labs.

And no ledges.

He eyed the windows. They were about eight meters
apart in straight up-and-down rows, and they had a
small sill, perhaps fifteen centimeters. He walked to
a middle row, gauged it, and jumped, reaching the
second window, uncertainly clinging to the sill by his
fingers.

He hoisted himself up, examined the room, a typical
hospital ward. It was empty. He started to break the
transparent material of the window, when he noticed a
shadow within. He ducked back down, peeking just in
the window.

A soldier entered, leading five others, blank-faced,
linked by a slender rope. As Daniel watched, they were
gently but forcefully pushed to the floor. The soldier
nodded in satisfaction, then left.

They were "thin" symbs, Daniel knew. Their im-
printed personality had faded, and they were mindless
automatons. Still, he decided not to risk entering this
room. They might still have a little flash of reaction,
and he'd rather not have to fight. He eyed the next
sill, then carefully pulled himself up on it. He looked
nervously at the symbs, but they seemed oblivious.

He judged distance, wind, atmospheric resistance, and the like, and made the leap. He almost missed it, grabbing the third-floor window with just four fingers of his right hand. Slowly he gained balance, and grip, and looked in.

The room was empty. He waited a few minutes to see if anyone would pass the door, but nobody did, and there were no shadows or noises. He decided to risk entry, applied power, and hit the window hard. It flexed, then gave, dropping loudly on the floor. It did not break, though. He waited a bit until he was satisfied that no one had heard, then hauled himself in. He went over to the open door and cautiously peered out. The hall seemed to be empty.

Slowly, cautiously, quietly, he started down the hall.

He'd only progressed halfway, finding all the rooms deserted, when the hospital P.A. barked to life.

"Not that way, Captain Daniel," the voice of a kindly old man echoed down the corridors. He froze, then turned. There was still no one in sight. He walked back up the other way.

"Nor that way, either, Captain," came the hollow voice again. "You'll never find her without help. Why don't you come up and talk with us? Use the lift about twenty meters further on. Come to the fourth-floor executive offices. We'll be waiting."

It was the Machist. He knew that, deep down. He'd been expected!

"Why should I trust you?" he called out to the walls, his own voice echoing slightly down the corridor.

"You shouldn't," replied the ghostly voice. "But, then again, what have you to lose? You're not really here, anyway—and we have the girl."

He sighed. The damned creature was right! If they knew where he was, they could zap him at will. And there was no risk to him—as the man said, he wasn't really here.

He walked over to the lift, and it opened for him automatically, as if it'd been waiting for him. It was empty, and he stepped in and pressed 4.

It irritated him that they seemed to know so much more about him than he knew about them.

The door opened in a few seconds, revealing an office complex. There was an empty reception desk, a blank wall, and a corridor off to the left. A partition and single door stood to the right. The sign on the door said: HOSPITAL DIRECTOR.

He turned right, opened the door, and walked in.

As befitted a top executive, it was a large, spacious office dominated by a huge desk and two chairs facing it. Behind the desk was a Ponder.

The Machist smiled broadly.

"Come in! Come in!" he invited. "We know it's silly, but sit down! You don't know how much we've looked forward to this little chat!"

He went over and took the seat, although it meant little to him. Force of habit.

"You're not the director of this little project," Daniel said softly. "You're just another symb."

The old man shrugged. "True, this is not our true form, but you'll meet us personally sooner or later, we promise you. Anyway, we're not talking to the real you, either, are we? We assure you the simile is apt; this particular vessel is an exact symb, unlike the programed, simple tools you have heretofore encountered."

"Where is she?" the Combine man asked coldly.

Ponder sighed. "Safe, we assure you. Alive, yes. Awaiting disposition instructions from you, really."

"Why you—" Daniel exclaimed angrily, and started to move to leap across the desk.

Ponder threw up his hands. "Wait a minute! What would it gain you to destroy a symb?"

Daniel froze. "Satisfaction," he snarled.

Ponder shrugged. "If you like, we can arrange for you to destroy a hundred thousand Ponders. We don't need them anymore."

The cold remark both appalled him and calmed him. He sat back down in the chair.

Ponder sighed. "We assure you that nothing will

happen until you have heard us out, and that she will not be killed in any case. Does that satisfy you?"

It did, a little.

"However," Ponder continued in that same infuriating fatherly tone, "we said the disposition is up to you. We mean it. Literally. If you will hear us out, you'll understand."

"Go ahead," he responded skeptically. "I'm listening."

Ponder smiled and leaned forward on his desk. "First, let's get rid of some of your questions. What this is all about."

"You realize, of course, that what you say also is eventually reported to the Combine," Daniel reminded him. Just a reminder to the other who was fighting whom.

"Yes, yes, we know," Ponder nodded. "After all, that's what this is all about. First, let us thank you for what you've done for us so far. The project would have been far more difficult without you."

Daniel started. *"What?"*

Ponder grinned. "Oh, we didn't *expect* you. Didn't know you existed, in fact, at the start. But, you see, we've been short-handed here since the beginning—terribly pressed for time—and you very nicely organized all those people in the bush and kept them out of our way for much of the time. They were a real nuisance at the beginning—one person in the bush, raiding our camps, shooting up things occasionally, tied up dozens, maybe up to a hundred soldiers. You rallied them nicely. Keep them cohesive, and away from our camps and our business. Oh, we had help from others, too, of course," he added cheerfully. "Sten Rolvag, for example. Did a wonderful job, particularly in this critical area. We helped all we could. A cache of medikits here, herding some game animals toward the caves with a flyer, and so forth."

Daniel was aghast. "You mean Rolvag was *cooperating* with you?" He'd known the man was a skunk, but this was beyond belief.

Ponder had a playful expression. "Well, no, not exactly. I think, deep down, he suspected he was being deliberately spared and helped, but he'd never admit it, even to himself. He had what he wanted, and we made certain that he continued to have it. That was one reason we didn't touch the observer radio network. It channeled all those refugees to camps like Rolvag's, where they could be controlled out of the way, and watched. One day, if time had permitted, we'd have taken them, of course, but that wasn't our paramount concern."

"And you didn't have enough time," Daniel shot back. "Right now I'm getting reports that you're losing, that your line is breaking. It won't be much longer."

That big grin was back. "But, we *did* have enough time, though barely," Ponder replied. "Again, partially thanks to you. We really did intend to evacuate as much as possible, so you caused some inconvenience there, but, either way, if you hadn't blown the pads we would have. It'll take them a month to get any kind of force on Ondine with portable pads and small shuttles. Most of them will be construction people, here to rebuild the pads. Another month, with the best automated machinery. By that time the last of the people's camps will be completed, and the final stage will be well along."

Daniel had a sudden, eerie feeling. "Final stage?" he repeated.

Ponder sat back in the big chair and put on his professorial manner. "This brings us," he began, "to what's going on here."

"To begin with," Ponder said, "let's start at the *real* beginning. The original Machists—really just a word we made up, not what we call ourselves—how you humans like labels!" He seemed to lose his train of thought, then got it back.

"Well, as we said, the original Machists came from a planet of enormous mass. They were just about held together by it. *Were,* in fact, which is why they had no real luck with space travel. Well, they went through the usual evolutionary steps, particularly socially, and they built a grand civilization. Stabilized their population at about five billion, provided for all their needs. A society of pure thought and research.

"But what do you do when you finally know everything you *can* know about your own planet and environment? You stagnate, or you strike out, explore. Our bodies, though—well, that's something we can't explain to you. There is no equivalent in your part of the universe. Or ours, either. Let's just say that every time we tried to send anything "organic" up, no matter how good its artificial gravity and environment, we just—well, broke apart. A pretty problem. They had to reach to the stars or stagnate, and the peculiar rules of their biology prohibited that."

Daniel was ahead of him. "But you sent machines out, didn't you? Some of your machines would hold together where your organic material wouldn't. That's why Machist—simply, 'machine.' "

Ponder nodded approvingly. "Yes, yes, that's it exactly! But that didn't solve our problem either. Distances are impossibly vast, and vaster still were the transmission times. Within a thousand light-year area, it was actually quicker to send the machines out and bring them back than to have them transmit data. But most didn't come back. They were all self-aware, of course, but we couldn't think of *everything*. So, research went on. The whole race fell to it, working on nothing else. And, of course, we found the answer. We found a way to mate our own minds to those of our machines, to literally *become* our machines.

"That's what the Machists are, Daniel. They're you."

Daniel sat silently for a few moments. The concept was staggering. Five billion people like him, each sealed in his own spaceship, for all time.

"The computer hardware is far more sophisticated than yours, of course," Ponder continued. "And the design concept was approached differently, but the end result is close enough."

Daniel looked at him. "So there are no Machists on this planet. You're in orbit somewhere, directing all this."

"At the moment," Ponder replied casually, "we're that rather large pitted red asteroid about three hundred meters off your port bow."

And, in his golden egg, Daniel looked and saw it. It was *huge*—more than four kilometers around. He'd seen it before, along with the thousands of other minor moons circling Ondine. He'd tracked them all, too, to avoid collisions. This one had been so subtle he'd not even noticed a slight orbital acceleration.

"How long have you been there?" he asked.

Ponder shrugged. "Not long. You're so small we could never have picked you out. Nonetheless, you are human in reactions—and we've studied human psychology long and well. When you knew we had the girl you became emotional, you thought of nothing else. That disguised our subtle course maneuvers, made on the other side, of course, out of sight. You should know that only a tiny difference will greatly vary an orbit."

"But—but how did you find me?" he stammered. "Out of those thousands of specks . . ." He shook his head in wonder.

"When your female symb was destroyed at the spaceport, we deduced that you would not abandon the girl. We made a slow show of loading her in the van. Frankly, we thought you'd rush the van, we could cut you down, and achieve the same result. You surprised us by turning noble and blowing the spaceport. Of course, we really *didn't* know where the symb was until you acted."

"You retracked the launch of this symb," he said, almost mechanically.

Ponder shrugged. "Easy when you know that there's to be a launch, can estimate the size of the object, and know its final destination. Ballistics is an exact science. When we computed your trajectory, it was child's play to find you by back tracking."

As they sat, Daniel tried a few maneuvers. The other object matched him, its targeting locked on. He could outdistance it easily if he could first break orbit —but if he started to do that, the thing would have him.

"I assume you're armed," he said.

In answer, the object, so like a pitted asteroid, sent two strong bursts just in front of him.

Daniel sighed. "So you have me. Would it surprise you to learn that it doesn't matter to me?"

Ponder's smile faded. "We're sorry to hear that, although we can sympathize. That, of course, makes the girl even more important, doesn't it?"

The mention of Amara upset him again. Ponder saw it, and threw his hands in the air. "Will you sit there and listen?" he pleaded. "This story isn't finished yet."

"I think I already understand more of it than you do," Daniel replied cryptically. His meaning sailed over the other's head, and Ponder continued.

"Now, as I say, can you imagine five billion people like yourself? Products of a utopian environment. We poked, we explored, and, finally, we ran into another race. A spacefaring race, yes, but not nearly at our level. We opened contact, we sent out symbs—in our image, of course—and we rejoiced that we'd found another race."

Ponder's expression clouded. "They feared us. They reacted violently at the very appearance of our symbs. They panicked at so many self-sustaining beings hovering off their planets. They attacked us! After a thousand years of wandering, we were attacked irrationally by the first intelligent beings we met! Well, naturally, we defended ourselves. It was a terrible mismatch, we were so far beyond them. And that left us with a large number of captive aliens.

"We experimented, poked, probed, and, we fear, made a lot of errors. But we learned! We had no alternative, other than to exterminate them!"

"You could have just gone your own way," Daniel retorted.

"And have a potential enemy in our backfield out for revenge? No, that wasn't possible. So, of course, we had to convert them, we had to make them think like us, become a biological analog of ourselves."

"Turn them into living machines, you mean," Daniel said disgustedly.

"No! No!" Ponder protested. "We made them like us, yes. We taught them to think communally, to live without hatred, lust, fear, distrust. A perfect society, but with emotion, with what you might call humanity. The *good* emotions. Love. Trust. Faith. Charity. Mercy. Compassion."

"The things you couldn't find anymore in yourselves," Daniel said softly.

Ponder nodded slowly. "In a way, of course, you are right. We were alone, isolated from one another, except by broadcast. We were of one mind and purpose and set of beliefs, but we could not share directly with one another. But *they* could! And *did!* Our methods worked on their scale as well or better than they did for us!"

Daniel shook his head sadly. "They're your children. That's the way you reproduce. The only way you can feel like real people again."

"It was a mission!" Ponder insisted. "When the second race we met reacted exactly like the first, we realized that we might be unique. They were creatures far, far different from the first group, but they shared the same animalism beneath the surface. They were a race in terrible emotional pain! We learned that the first methods didn't work on another alien species, and we had to adapt them, but we eventually revolutionized the second race as well. And the third. And so on. Thousands of races, now! In one glorious utopian system!"

Daniel felt ill. "Trillions of monuments to your vain attempt to overcome the loneliness and isolation that traps and drives you."

Ponder sighed in frustration. Their minds were definitely not meeting. Each rejected the other's vision.

"And, finally," Daniel continued, "you ran into the humans and the Combine. And, after some early successes based on surprise, you ran up against a stone wall."

Ponder nodded agreement. "The largest civilization we'd ever seen, ever come across. And technologically amazing. We are still learning how amazing. You, for example, are a form we would never have expected to run across. You are, in fact, the greatest threat we ever faced."

This remark piqued Daniel's curiosity. "Go on," he invited.

"We foresee humanity's eventually building more and more of you, in ever more sophisticated models. An animalistic analog of the Machist culture! The damage it would cause! The havoc! Even though we began the Ondine project without knowledge of your kind, you more than justified it.

Daniel thought carefully before saying, "I still don't see it. If there are five billion of you, you could still punch us to hell."

Ponder calmed down. "Oh, that's a mental figure. Actually, there are only ten thousand of us. Not all here, of course. Not at all. In the main the Machists in this battle are from other worlds."

Daniel gasped. "There are a *hundred thousand* minds in that ship of yours?"

"Well, yes," the Machist replied. "We weren't very large to begin with, you see."

"Then minds *can* be mated in the cyborg linkups!" Daniel exclaimed excitedly.

Ponder was cautious. "Well, yes and no. Frankly, if you place just two independent minds in one link, they'll malfunction. One wants to go left, you see, and the other right. And so on, to the infinitely complex, no matter how close they are personally. The only solution is a total mating of the minds. A total

merging of identity, of self, so you have one mind
that is the sum of all its parts."

Daniel sighed. There went *that* dream. "That explains the camps," he said softly. "The total lack of
self-identity in the group."

Ponder nodded. "The meld is essential to the concept. It's achieved in different ways, not only with each
race but with each group of individuals within a race,
but the end is *always* attainable. Frankly, for such a
great, strong race, your psyches are remarkably vulnerable. Perhaps it *is* because you are so far along. You
are ready for this stage, you need it to match your
material greatness."

Daniel shook his head. "No, I think you have it
wrong. We are great *because* of our pain. Our newest,
most radical developments occur as the result of things
like wars. That's why we're holding our own now,
and gaining on you. That's why we'll *win*. Every time
you induce your social utopia on a people they become machines, able to function, able to do their
jobs, even happy, but *stagnant*. I'll bet you that no
convert Machist has come up with a new invention, a
new concept of any kind. Any advancement you
achieve is an idea stolen from a race you conquer.
And if you can't steal these ideas by continuing to conquer, then you'll stagnate to the core. We'll eat you
alive."

Ponder stared at him in a mixture of pity and wonder.
"But, what is the point of progress if the only way to
sustain it is for the bulk of the people to be miser-
able?" he asked softly.

And there it was. The basic dichotomy that made
the Machists alien to human culture.

For both, in their own way, were absolutely correct
—and absolutely opposed.

"Maybe there isn't any point to existence," Daniel
responded. "Maybe the religions are right. They provide
the point. Maybe they're wrong. Maybe there is no
point to any of this. But, we will never agree. The
debate will go to the strongest, which, I believe, will

be humanity in the end, and humanity for sure in a matter of hours or a day at most on Ondine."

Ponder sighed. "Ondine. Ah, yes."

"Why did you do this to Ondine?" Daniel asked quietly.

"We're in stalemate," Ponder replied. "You know it, we know it. Thirteen years with no gains, nothing for us except a conviction in the rightness of our cause. To break it, without huge cost, we needed an example. A place that could be quickly converted to our way, then given back. A demonstration of our system, and a place for all the Combine to see just how morally and psychologically weak you are. A resort—so well known that our work here couldn't be ignored. The press will be with the first landing party. Word will get back even if they try and censor it. People will come, study our system and its results. Reaction can go one of two ways, either to our benefit. It will win converts, open up talks leading to a melding of races, or it will cause massive demoralization, encourage all who know the weaknesses and sickness inside your own souls and your societies to try and change it. Such social disruption will weaken the war effort, perhaps force an accommodation."

So that was it. Seven million dead, nine million changed into something alien. Merely a demonstration. A showpiece. A propaganda gimmick.

"Will you tell me," Daniel asked, "how you got three hundred fifty thousand symbs on this planet so fast?"

Ponder grinned. "Why, in the first few worlds we captured we learned Combine economics. Nine years ago we established a trading company using symbs disguised as humans. Since the symbs all replaced real people, nobody suspected. Slowly, we introduced some Machist products. One of the ironies is that virtually all of Ondine's publicity posters and promos were produced by us. With the profits we bought materials, made symbs. A number were brought to our Ondine offices in every one of our freighters. As for the last—well, it was Ondine's peak season. Our symbs simply walked into travel agencies in small groups all over the Combine and *bought tickets!*"

Daniel shook his head disbelievingly. "They were here all the time—ahead of time. And converted into soldiers for the takeover."

Ponder nodded. "And half into Ponders when the camps were secured. We might say we're stretched thin, were even more so in the beginning. That was why we had to have the energy barriers at the start, and why it took some time to get around to all the camps with the teaching phase. The same symbs had to be reused."

"I think you've lost your investment," Daniel told him. "I think you'll find humanity will be collectively outraged at your callousness toward life and at your treatment of individual humans as objects."

Ponder looked surprised. "Why? It's only a matter of degree, you know. Most humans are callous about others unless unpleasantness directly touches them. We'll bet many people cheer when they read that two Combine ships were lost but three Machist ships were destroyed. And everyone—your government, business-es, and even most people, treat other people as objects. They want people to listen to and minister to *their* problems, but few have time or inclination to consider the problems of the people they want to listen to them. As we say, a matter of degree only." He looked at Daniel coldly. "Would *you* be here, now, if it was some *other* man or woman we held?"

There was a flaw in his reasoning, someplace. He was sure of it. But, perhaps, he thought, the flaw is in man. It didn't matter. "All you say is irrelevant. We'll soon be retaking Ondine," he told the Machist.

Ponder smiled. "No, and yes. You will retake the property, but *we* will retain the *people.*"

Daniel felt a sinking sensation again. "What do you mean by that?"

"Ondine has not been properly utilized," Ponder

replied. "Now it will be. You must have noticed the physical changes in the people."

Daniel nodded, starting to see.

"You must have realized that such changes cannot come about in so short a time naturally. From the start we gave them a series of injections. Some, it's true, contained the disease-prevention agents, but they also contained something else, specially formulated for Ondine."

He reached in a desk drawer, took out a vial. "Your scientists will analyze this. You were fools to outlaw genetic research on humans. You have been expanding backward. You don't adapt the planet to the people, you adapt the people to the planet." Ponder replaced the vial, and smiled. "That's what *we* do," he said smugly.

"What does *it* do?" Daniel asked quietly, but nervously.

"It's a clever little agent," Ponder replied. "It goes round and round and gets into every cell in the body. The exercises help, of course, but basically it tells the genes to do different things, and it does it at a fast rate, much faster than normal. Some, like the inland colonists, are turning into redesigned humanity. You may have noticed how similar they looked. Within another year, they will be absolutely identical, as identical outside as they are inside. Strong—strong enough to be a match for your symbs. Tough—so tough broken bones will be scarce. All injuries will heal quickly. A good deal of autoregeneration is provided. Resistant to most known diseases. Able to digest almost *any* vegetable matter, which their redesigned mouths will handle well. And sexless. Each will bear one child, breeding true, and be able to nurse it. And age? They'll keep their bodies for an Ondinian century, then simply die and rapidly decompose. They'll be cold-blooded, too, so they will be able to tolerate any extremes of Ondinian temperature."

Daniel looked at him glumly. "You said the inland ones," he noted.

Ponder nodded enthusiastically. "Of course! Ondine is eighty-three percent ocean. The bulk of the population will, after a while, find itself impelled to the sea, a genetic migration. They will look like nothing remotely human, but they will have the same advantages as the land people."

"We can reverse the process," Daniel said stubbornly.

"We suppose you could," Ponder admitted. "After it's complete. Before then reversal would kill them. But you won't. By that time they will be so nonhuman the Combine won't want to invest the time and money. You see, humans reject alien species. You fear them, detest them. That's why this genetic experimentation was outlawed. The fear that they'd come up with something inhuman—which, in early experiments, we think they did. Your whole history is one of hatred of others who were different, even slightly so. Race, color, language, whatever. No, your leaders will fear these, and might even exterminate all of them, perhaps providing the ultimate proof that our way is the best way."

"I'll see that they're not," Daniel told him. "Now where's the girl?"

Ponder sat up in his chair. "The girl again. Well, let's get to that as the last thing. Right now we have the girl and we have you—the real you—in our sights. You will choose your own fate, and by that, choose hers as well."

"What have you done with her?" Daniel demanded.

"Here are your choices. We have made them as simple for you as we can. You can join us. We will redesign your onboard sections to make you greater than you are now. And, we will assist you and the girl in Machist principles, achieving, eventually, a mind-meld that will permit the installation of you both in your vessel."

Daniel thought of the brainwashed group he'd encountered on the way to Lamarine. Even if the Machists could work the same transformation on Amara and himself, they wouldn't be the same people. They'd be alien, as alien as those people in the camps, alien in mind as he was in body.

"And if I refuse?" he replied calmly.

"Well, we shall destroy you, of course. And if that does not trouble you, you will abandon the girl in so doing to a much more horrible fate."

He had that sinking feeling again. "What have you done to her?"

"If she is to be mated to you in Machist union, she has no further need for her body," Ponder noted calmly. "What we did was surgically complete the trimming you so casually began. Additionally, we introduced an agent that is cousin to, but much simpler than, that in the vial we showed you. It's a simple mutative retardant. It will not harm her in any way, but she will never be able to regrow what has been lost. Regeneration will not take. She will remain the way she is now—and remarkably healthy, too, since that is a byproduct of the cellular agent—for the rest of her probably long life."

"You son of a bitch," Daniel said, all emotion drained from him. He knew now how they worked, how they won converts. *Every* human, even he, had a weakness. If death would not coerce you, they had other ways of forcing their decision on you. He would like to transmit this conversation and die. He could never have her, and he could not live without her. And yet, they'd stolen her future as surely as they had that of the other people on Ondine.

The Machists would have him—who they wanted, if only to see what the human techs had come up with that might be of use to them—and her, as one Machist true-believer unit. Or he would condemn her to a living hell.

No wonder the bastard had been so confident!

And yet, and yet, he thought grimly, even faced with such a choice as this we are not the masters of our own fate.

"It's too late, Machist," he told Ponder in a hollow

tone. "There is no longer a decision for me to make. Perhaps if this choice had been given me at the start, you would have won." He saw Ponder's grin fade, and it gave him some measure of satisfaction. "But I've done the job. *I've stalled you in conversation long enough.* If you'll look off *your* port bow, and stern, and just above a bit, you'll see the Combine heavy cruisers *Dagger*, *Messenger*, and *Sword*, who rushed here through the breach I already knew was there before I came here. I signaled that you were holding me disguised as an asteroid. I've been hoping to stall you long enough, and I did. Remember those ship names, Ponder? They were all heavily damaged, with many losses, in the battle in which you took Ondine. Their crews lost many friends in that. They're itching to shoot all hundred thousand of you back into your primal energy form. I couldn't join you if I wanted to, now—and I couldn't rescue the girl."

"No!" Ponder screamed. He jumped to his feet, eyes blazing. "But you'll have suffered as the rest do not!" he threatened in maniacal triumph.

"Where's the girl, Ponder?" he asked again.

"In the lobby of the Alemartre Hotel," he snarled. "You'll enjoy our little display there. The other side of the propaganda message."

Daniel got up calmly, leaving the other standing there. He reached the door, then turned. "Who's the animal, now, Ponder?" he asked quietly. "Hatred? Triumph in revenge?" He sighed. "Good-bye, Ponder." He walked out the door.

Daniel walked down the corridor to the elevator, and as he did he witnessed the final act.

The great Machist asteroid opened fire. The three ships returned it almost instantly, pouring enormous chunks of raw energy into the mountainous mass.

A shot was directed in the direction of the golden egg, but he was ready for it, and back near *Messenger* too fast for them. They had bigger problems. Or, perhaps, he thought grimly, they were having their final revenge. They were condemning him to live.

The mass broke for freespace, but the relentless energy pouring into it was breaking it apart. It split, revealing a weird honeycomblike interior before breaking into fragments which quickly fell prey to Ondine's gravity.

Faster the Machists fell, and faster still. The Combine ships pursued as close as they dared to ensure the breakup of the larger chunks.

They were burning now, a great meteor shower spectacular to behold from space, but hidden from ground view by Ondine's ever-present cloud cover.

"They're withdrawing!" he heard someone from Command call. "Pulling back all along the line. We've done it!"

Someone on *Dagger* sighed on the tactical channel.

"I guess that's it, then," he said.

And everyone on the ships involved cheered wildly and embraced, and cried with joy.

All but one lonely figure walking down the Lamarine boardwalk.

Tenero

THE MACHIST DISPLAY WAS CRUEL INDEED. FIRST, there was a sign over the big doors that said: WELCOME HEROES! He pushed open the great doors and stepped inside.

It was a museum of horrors. Mutilated bodies in terrible poses, surgically and chemically altered specimens that were grotesque in the extreme. Pictures and 'visor stuff on the stages of the transformation of the population, so that no doubt would be left as to who did it to whom. No way to claim that the people here now were different creatures from the original population, substitutes.

And one terribly cruel living exhibit.

They had her by herself, facing the door, mercifully unable to see the displays behind her. It was the same beautiful face, the same lovely breasts and torso, even the long black hair.

But that was all. They had taken everything they could without killing her, and used the superior hospital equipment to make it seem she was born that way.

She was the last casualty of the Battle of Ondine.

She was set in a plastic stand with a form-fitted brace. She'd been dozing, but awoke when she heard the doors slide open. He walked in, and at first she didn't recognize him. Then, suddenly, she remembered the face of that first visitor to Rolvag's caves, and the manner, the walk.

"H-i," she managed, softly, shyly embarrassed, unable to do anything, even hide, even kill herself.

He walked over to her, the sadness and pity in his own mind having no outlet in his machine body.

"I—I come to a point now," she tried, looking down, voice quivering. Tears welled up in her, and she tried to look away from him for a moment.

"I'm sorry," was all he could say.

She looked back at him, tears still flowing. "They told me about it. Even laughed about it. I guess you told them to go to hell with their deal. I prayed you would."

He didn't tell her how close he'd come to accepting. "I had no choice," he replied. "The Combine located the Machists in orbit and killed them."

"I'm glad." She nodded, trying to compose herself. "I—I could never have stood being turned into creatures like we saw in the camp. Turning *you* into one. Creatures who could do that—" She paused for a moment as more tears came, then continued. "Even *this* is better than that. Better my limbs than my mind."

Some hair fell in her eyes and she shook her head violently to get it away. It was the only moving part she'd been left.

She looked at him again. "Th-they said I'd always be like this. That they'd fixed it so nothing would work, not regeneration, not cloning, not even robotic connectors."

He went over to her, braced her back with his hand, and kissed her, long and hard. "We'll see, Princess," he said gently. "Either way, we still have a job to do. What they've done to Ondine is worse than anything you could have imagined. We're going to have to save the colonists from our own people, and help these new varieties of humanity to adjust to their new world and to ours."

"It's a big job," she responded.

"Well, I'll do the walking and you'll do the feeling, and together we'll make a whole person," he told her. He looked around at the ghastly exhibit.

"Let me get you out of this chamber of horrors," he said, and lifted her gently. On impulse, he picked up the stand as well.

He held her gently in his left arm, facing her forward so she could see what he did, and walked out the door.

The tough marine medical officer looked at him, and at Amara, and he wanted to alternately cry and throw up. He managed to do neither. He took Daniel aside.

"They did it, all right," he almost whispered. "Shot her so full of the stuff it had no problems. What it does, it seems, is change the genetic and neural codes almost constantly. The cells alter just a little, but it's enough to make regeneration or sophisticated prosthesis impossible. A fast clone was tried, and it didn't live an hour. The robot prosthetics won't work because they depend on each nerve to do the same thing every time. The best we can do is a voice-activated robot, which would contain her, which she could move in, and which could attend to minimal bodily functions. And yet, the same little bits of protein and other molecules that are doing this to her devour harmful agents at a fantastic rate, even common poisons. I'd say that short of electrocution she might easily live another seventy years, maybe longer."

Daniel nodded. "I'll break it to her," he said gently, and the chief medical officer looked enormously thankful.

Amara had already resigned herself to her fate, and so the news didn't come as a great shock, but its finality was deadening.

"Shall I order that robot?" he asked her.

She nodded. "Yes, but not for the camps and the bush. I'll trust you for that. You've seen how it helps in talking to them. The bush people lose all their self-pity, and the camp people accept me as one of them, something I wouldn't be with a blinking, whirring machine around me."

He nodded. "Okay. Agreed."

She looked up at him, and smiled, genuinely. "You remember that first camp we went into? How that one—ah, member—came up to us, looked at me, and asked if someone like me had a job?"

"I remember," he replied.

"And I realized then that I *did* have a job—a purpose is what she really meant. And in that moment, I knew I *did* have a purpose, like this. I was the bridge between them and humanity. Only like *this* was it possible. I am a creature, like the camps and sea people. Someone they can identify with. Made alien, like them, by the Machists. And that's the way the humans react. Like I'm a different creature. Only, unlike the Ondinians, I can talk to them as a person. And those in the bush—if *I* can adjust, *they* can adjust. It's almost as if it were planned that way."

He kissed her, and held her to him.

"Besides," she said, "I get the best-looking man on Ondine."

"All seventeen of him," he agreed.

AUTHOR KILLED IN FREAK ACCIDENT

LAMARINE, ONDINE 7-3 (UPF). Amara Schtinik, noted author of books on alien sociology, psychology, and poetry, was struck by lightning and died instantly on the Lamarine boardwalk just a little under four years after the liberation of Ondine. A Machist-deformed quadraplegic, she often used a voice-actuated robot while in Lamarine, and authorities at Ondine Naval Command indicated that the robot drew the lightning. Schtinik, a hero to billions across the Combine for her refusal to accept her physical limitations as a handicap, was chief architect and supervisor for the Ondine restoration and a leader in the fight to protect the Machist-altered population from extermination or exploitation. The former marine is survived by her husband, Commodore Daniel, Commander of the Ondine District. She was 23.

Coda

*Clap! Clap! Step! Step! Lock step! Pivot step! Kick!
Kick! Kick!*

The people have come in from the fields; it is just
past sunset now, and they gather ritually after the
evening meal to celebrate the fullness of the day by
doing the dance of sharing.

*Step! Bend! Step! Bend! Walk! Walk! Back! Walk!
Right foot, paw! Paw! Paw!*

"Of course our presence has disturbed the established mind-set," the psychologist says to the VIPs
watching the dancers along the coast.

"Can't you just shatter the whole conditioning?"
a military officer growls. "Why permit this bullshit
to continue?"

The psychologist shuffles uncomfortably. The
military mind's unbending tendency to reduce all people
to ciphers and solve all problems by direct force is
the hardest problem in the reclamation project.

"You've got to understand, sir," the psychologist
tries, "that it just isn't that simple. Everyone has some
problem, some weakness. The psychologists of the
Machists exploited this. Most people are not really
happy. That's why religious cults, social experiments,
and even lonely hearts clubs thrive. Our own mush-
rooming suicide rate shows how vulnerable we are."

"You mean," the military man responds in an amazed tone, "they like it better the way they are?"

The psychologist smiles humorlessly. "Let us just say that they find it preferable to what they care to remember about their past lives. They couldn't go back, anyway. Their genetic codes have been altered. With seven years in the tanks we could remake them into humans, but only out of a catalog. And even if we could return them to their former state, their experiences will have made them totally alien inside. Yes, the Machists did their job, they changed nine million into truly alien lifeforms—but not *Machist* aliens."

"What do you mean?" asks another, a politician.

"Because the Machist system is ultimately dependent on the absence of alternatives," the psychologist explains patiently. "The final insurance they have is that the people know that they must join the new system or die. Most will join under those circumstances. Now, with us in charge, they have options, alternatives. Many of the groups are already changing socially, and there will be more as time goes on if we make certain we don't force the issue, but keep those options open."

"And the sea people?" a bureaucratic type asks.

"No difference," the psychologist tells him, "except that they will evolve socially and develop radically different from the land people. They'll make it, though, and give us an incredible opportunity to see how human minds react in alien surroundings."

Lock step! Pivot step! Turn! Turn! Turn!

The man looks human, but everyone knows he is not. He is the most familiar human face on Ondine, and he walks past the dancers at their pleasure and gives a friendly smile and a wave in their direction. The dancers in the afterglow do not break rhythm, but do introduce a kind of bow into their prancing.

The man's expression is one of satisfaction, his manner one of confidence and good humor. There is nothing in his placid exterior to show the million psychic swords slicing at the very core of his being.

He reaches the shore, where a small one-man fishing boat is tied to a makeshift pier, jumps aboard, and starts the little motor. Its *pip, pip, pip,* cannot be heard over the chants of the dancers and the roar of the surf. The man aims for that rapidly vanishing afterglow, alone on a darkly painted sea, a single, tiny figure chasing a sun that has already deserted him.

Far overhead, a small, golden egg-shaped object fires three short bursts that jar it out of orbit, and it begins to move.

Lock step! Pivot step! Twirl! Twirl! Twirl!

"I still don't like it," the military man growls. "Between the rockheads and the squids this whole damn place gives me the creeps!"

"That's why we never did such things ourselves," the psychologist tells him. "The potential and knowledge of what it could do in the wrong hands stopped all such research. Now we are faced with it whether we want it or not. I'd like to think we've matured enough to use it wisely. It is an awesome power—and a terrible responsibility."

"They're already saying the technique is cheaper and better than terraforming," the politician notes. "Within our lifetimes, I fear, the term human may lose its meaning."

The bureaucrat decides to step in. "That's why this is so important a project," he emphasizes. "Remember, the war continues. As we slowly gain superiority, we will be taking Machist worlds, worlds that weren't even human to begin with, and Lord knows what after the Machists got through with them. We can't exterminate the whole galaxy, you know. We have to learn to deal with them as effectively as the Machists learned how to deal with us."

They stand in silence a moment as the dancers continue.

"This used to be one hell of a beautiful place," the military man growls at last.

"Still is, sir, still is," the psychologist replies without

looking away from the dancers. "It just isn't ours any-more. It's *theirs*."

Link! Twirl! Link! Twirl! Step! Step! Back step! Pivot step!

The man in the boat is alone now on a quiet sea. It is a little choppy, but he doesn't seem to mind. Near-by, suddenly, there is a splash and a gurgle, and two of the sea people surface and stare at him. He gives them the regulation smile and wave, but, strangely, they do not respond, just keep staring at him.

His eyes, so unlike human eyes, can see others of their kind swimming in shared togetherness, looping, whirling, playing, celebrating life in their own way as the dancers are on the shore.

"Daniel! Daniel!" calls a voice inside him. "You have broken orbit. Explain, please. You are drifting in-system. Can you explain nature of difficulty?"

Yes, he thinks sadly. *I can explain the nature of the difficulty. But you wouldn't understand it—or be able to help if you did.*

The wounds, those terrible wounds, scars on his soul, flare anew at the thought, strengthening his resolve still further.

He notes they are putting an intercept on him, and he boosts at full power toward the bright, glowing, growing object ahead of him, the star Arachnus, bath-ing Ondine with warmth and light.

The two sea people are suddenly alarmed. The man is standing now at the bow of the little boat, arms outstretched to the darkening horizon, seeming to reach for something indefinable beyond their vision.

And then, even more strangely, he seems to do a few small dance steps.

Walk, walk, walk! Pivot step! Turn! Clap! Clap! Link!

The VIPs are watching the last of the dance.

"Funny," says one. "I know how hot it is, but for some reason I'm feeling chilly."

"How about a few drinks?" the admiral suggests. "The Marquis has reopened, you know."

"Terrific!" the politician enthuses. "We can make a real party out of it. I could go for some good old-fashioned *human* fun right now."

They start off toward the boardwalk. The dance is almost over anyway.

Kick! Kick! Step! Kick! Jump! Jump! CLAP!

The dance is over now. The people, laughing, prepare for sleep.

A little over a kilometer out in the dark ocean, the sea people watch, concerned, as the last dancer in the afterglow suddenly stiffens and falls woodenly into the embrace of the cool, silent sea.

About the Author

JACK L. CHALKER was born in Norfolk, Virginia, on December 17, 1944, but was raised and has spent most of his life in Baltimore, Maryland. He learned to read almost from the moment of entering school, and by working odd jobs had amassed a large book collection by the time he was in junior high school, a collection now too large for containment in his present quarters. Science fiction, history, and geography all fascinated him early on, interests which continue.

Chalker joined the Washington Science Fiction Association in 1958 and began publishing an amateur SF journal, *Mirage,* in 1960. After high school he decided to be a trial lawyer, but money problems and the lack of a firm caused him to switch to teaching. He holds B.S. degrees in history and English, and an M.L.A. from the Johns Hopkins University. He has taught history and geography in the Baltimore public schools since 1966, but is now writing full-time. Additionally, out of the amateur journals he founded a publishing house, The Mirage Press, Ltd., devoted to nonfiction and bibliographic works on science fiction and fantasy. This company has produced more than twenty books in the last eight years. His hobbies include working on science-fiction convention committees, guest lecturing on SF to institutions like the Smithsonian, esoteric audio, and travel. He is an active conservationist and National Parks supporter, and he has an intensive love of ferryboats, with the avowed goal of riding every ferry in the world. He is single, and still lives and works in Baltimore.